VANISHING MAPS

VANISHING MAPS

Cristina García

Alfred A. Knopf
New York • 2023

Grateful acknowledgment is made to New Directions Publishing Corp. for
permission to reprint an excerpt from "Romance Sonámbulo/ Somnambulist
Ballad" from *The Selected Poems of Federico García Lorca,* by Federico
García Lorca, translated by Stephen Spender and J. L. Gili, copyright © 1955
by New Directions Publishing Corp. Reprinted by permission of
New Directions Publishing Corp.

Library of Congress Cataloging-in-Publication Data
Names: García, Cristina, 1958– author.
Title: Vanishing maps: a novel / Cristina García.
Description: First Edition. | New York: Alfred A. Knopf, 2023.
Identifiers: LCCN 2022043000 (print) | LCCN 2022043001 (ebook) |
ISBN 9780593534748 (hardcover) | ISBN 9780593534755 (ebook)
Subjects: LCGFT: Novels.
Classification: LCC PS3557.A66 V36 2023 (print) |
LCC PS3557.A66 (ebook) |
DDC 813/.54—dc23/eng/20220909
LC record available at https://lccn.loc.gov/2022043000
LC ebook record available at https://lccn.loc.gov/2022043001

Jacket illustrations: flower © Yevheniia Bondarets/iStock/Getty Images;
cigarette in ashtray © Irina Griskova/iStock/Getty Images
Jacket design by John Gall

Manufactured in the United States of America

First Edition

To Gary, beloved

No border holds forever . . .

—GÜNTER GRASS

Family Tree

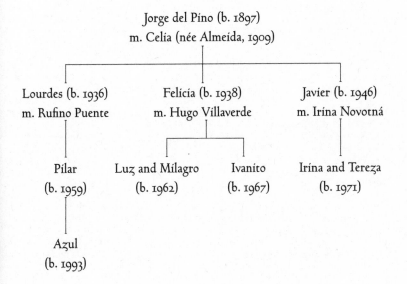

Jorge del Pino (b. 1897)
m. Celia (née Almeida, 1909)

Lourdes (b. 1936)
m. Rufino Puente

Felicia (b. 1938)
m. Hugo Villaverde

Javier (b. 1946)
m. Irina Novotná

Pilar
(b. 1959)

Luz and Milagro
(b. 1962)

Ivanito
(b. 1967)

Irina and Tereza
(b. 1971)

Azul
(b. 1993)

(1999-2000)

Ivanito Villaverde

Berlin

It was past midnight and the crowd was clamoring for their diva. At Chez Schatzi, everyone danced with whomever they pleased. Tonight was another coming-out party, a flagrant parade of secrets. Life was more alluring when they drank, when they got high, when they swayed as one. Last New Year's Eve, when La Ivanita dragged a jewel-encrusted ball and chain onstage, she'd incited a riot of rejoicing. For this and much more she was beloved in ravenous, after-hours Berlin.

Backstage La Ivanita put the finishing touches on her makeup: thickly angled eyeliner, iridescent powder, a slip of pink gloss on her lips. She adjusted her wig and smoothed the satin pleats of her vintage strapless gown. For the past four months she'd been rehearsing a playlist of Olga Guillot's sultriest boleros—"Miénteme," "Te Amaré Toda la Vida," "Total"—until her lip-synching was flawless. Guillot was her latest muse, a half-Jewish diva, a genius of gesture and melodrama, who'd enthralled Cuba in the fifties. Her voice drifted up from the turntable, which was perched next to a crystal bowl brimming with tangerines.

La Ivanita appraised herself in the gilded full-length mirror, a flea-market find. The vendor had flaunted its pedigree but she'd bargained him down to twenty marks flat. A reproduction of Otto Dix's

Metropolis hung on the wall behind her, its central panel luridly visible in the mirror. She placed three caramels and a shot glass of schnapps on her tiny santería altar, which was flickering with votive candles.

A flash of movement over her shoulder distracted her. La Ivanita turned around, vertebrae cracking, and scrutinized the tangle of glittering costumes in which her fans occasionally hid. She dreamed of finding her Russian dancer there—a god of a man!—with whom she'd enjoyed a swoony affair years ago. Ay, her testicles ached just thinking about him!

As she faced the mirror again, a thumb-size turbulence, like a speck of thundercloud, rotated in the upper left-hand corner. The thundercloud grew three-dimensionally, shooting off miniature lightning bolts, then floated directly into her sight line, as if daring La Ivanita to defy its existence. It was from this vortex that her mother emerged or, rather, the ghost of her did—lumpy and sleepy-eyed and wrapped in what looked like a World War II parachute, its edges frayed with red thread.

La Ivanita was stunned. She tried to speak but her throat closed off and her whole body trembled. Was she hallucinating?

Her mother shifted incrementally, turned in place to show off her camouflage. La Ivanita didn't know where to focus as the colors blended and whirled. Mami opened her mouth and emitted a low rasping sound, as if trying to rip the fibrous membrane dividing the living from the dead. *Imagination, like memory, can transform lies to truth,* she used to say. Is that what was happening here? A brazen rearranging of reality?

Before La Ivanita could utter a word, Mami vanished through the same knot in the universe from which she'd appeared. Only the spectral scent of gardenias betrayed that anything unusual had occurred.

The opening notes to Guillot's "Miénteme" reverberated through the theater. La Ivanita felt shaky but she'd worked too hard to call off this show. She pushed aside the leather curtain of her dressing room and glided onto the proscenium in sequined heels. The spotlight transformed her dazzling white gown into an even more dazzling blue. The piano fell reverentially silent. Waiters were fixed in place, silver trays suspended. Fanciful cocktails froze in midair. La Ivanita raised her arms and welcomed the worshipful roar of her fans.

Yes, this was her private chapel.

Voy viviendo ya de tus mentiras
sé que tu cariño no es sincero.
Sé que mientes al besar
y mientes al decir te quiero . . .

HAVANA

I

Celia del Pino

Havana

Celia del Pino woke up fiercely thirsty in the ice-cold bed. The blinds were half-open, inviting the last strips of moonlight into her room. If she strained to listen, she could hear the scratching of the late-shift nurse's pen, an injured cement worker's moaning (his thumb crushed in an industrial accident), a lonely cricket singing for its mate. Neon lines pulsed on the beeping monitor at her side, recording her every breath and heartbeat. There was a sharp twinge in the crook of her elbow, where the IV had been snugly taped. Her hands felt arthritic. She reached for the glass of water on her nightstand and accidentally spilled half of it on her hospital gown.

Celia patted herself dry with the thin blanket, then rearranged it over her knees. There was little left of her to create much of a topography beneath the unraveling cotton—just sunken planes and boney angles, the painful mound of her belly, a single shriveled breast. Her room, a stark enameled white, reminded her of the Russian refrigerator she'd been awarded once for exemplary service to the Revolution.

It was barely dawn. Two flies circled lazily overhead, as if through honey. Celia's vision blurred, then grew inexplicably telescopic. From her window she caught glimpses of Havana's patchwork rooftops, its illegal antennae, laundry lines crisscrossing the crumbling balconies. A viejita played solitaire at her kitchen table, a clay pot of lilies at her feet. The ocean wasn't visible but Celia smelled it like she could smell her own fermenting flesh.

A gentle hand on her brow disrupted her reveries. It was Reinaldo, the kind morning nurse, who'd come to take her temperature. Celia's fever remained high and her intestinal infection was pernicious despite the deluge of antibiotics. Her diverticula remained dangerously inflamed. One of them had ruptured, the doctors said, partly spilling the contents of her colon into her abdominal cavity. Sepsis had set in. For the last five days Celia had been flirting with death, semiconscious, dizzy from the drugs and unfamiliar faces.

Reinaldo gave her a dozen pills and a cup of diluted orange juice to wash them down.

"You know I can't even swallow an aspirin," Celia rasped.

"Go ahead, just one at a time. I have a prize for you when you finish."

Celia trusted this nurse. He was a good son of the Revolution, never any talk of abandoning the island, of living like El Rey de los Gusanos in Miami. She swallowed the first pill without trouble, choked on the second and third. Reinaldo refilled her cup halfway. It was only for the sweetness of the orange juice that she finished. The nurse rewarded Celia with a sheet of paper and a ballpoint pen.

"To write back to that lover of yours," he teased her. "You're never too old for romance!"

"Nonsense." Celia was pleased but tried not to show it. "And what about that cigar you promised me?" She took up smoking after El Líder had quit fourteen years ago, as if to continue the pleasure for him, as if to say, *I'll take the risk for you, guapo—no te preocupes.*

"That's going to be a lot harder." Reinaldo laughed and tucked a nub of gardenia-scented soap into Celia's battered handbag.

"Gracias, niño. You must be convinced that I'm going to make it out of here alive."

"Alive and squeaky clean," the nurse sang as he headed out the door. "So, write to him already! You won't be kicking around for-ever!"

It'd been weeks since Gustavo's first letter arrived, after an inex-plicable months-long journey from Spain, damaged and multiply-stamped, a half-dozen pages of oniony airmail paper translucent as her own skin. Another had followed just yesterday. Herminia had delivered it to Celia in the hospital, along with a batch of her malanga fritters.

"Now, don't go planning your funeral yet," her neighbor joked, handing over the Spaniard's letter. "Go ahead and read it. Late love is better than no love at all!"

Even the normally levelheaded Herminia had gotten caught up in the delusion of a romantic revival. Hadn't life taught her anything? Why wasn't she angry instead that Gustavo had dared unsettle Celia after a lifetime of radio silence? The arrogance of that man to expect his overtures to prevail—and at his convenience! As if his pesky ardor could resurrect Celia's love.

What Gustavo deserved was her scorn, a steaming helping of it! Celia had been infinitely more at peace when she'd believed her ex-lover dead. Over the years she'd relied on the solace of amnesia and a diminishing litany of regrets. What good were his words to her now? If Gustavo had never stopped loving her, as he professed, why had he chosen to spend his life without her? And the nerve of him to quote García Lorca, knowing exactly which lines would melt her heart!

Against her better judgment, Celia conjured up memories of Gustavo, flash-frozen in time, from their four rapturous nights at the Hotel Inglaterra. Bueno, there was no denying his beauty, his seductiveness. She could linger on a detailed inventory of his gifts, but it was his lips Celia remembered best. How they'd searched for the softness, the pleasure she had hidden even from herself.

I burned in your body / without knowing whose it was . . .

Gustavo hadn't promised her anything—that much was true—but

their flesh had made its own pledges. Didn't that count for something? Celia smoothed the sheet of paper on her food tray, uncapped the ballpoint pen, and began to write:

> *Querido Gustavo, It's been an eternity since I sent you my one and only letter. Did you ever receive it? I still know it by heart. A fish swims in my lung. Without you, what is there to celebrate?*

The cadaverous gastroenterologist swept into the room with a gaggle of interns. How young they looked, mere schoolboys! One had a cowlick. Another's stethoscope appeared oversize, as if he'd stolen it from a real doctor's medicine bag. And their voices were alternately hoarse and squeaking. How could they possibly be physicians? The clock on the wall ticked loudly, a reminder that their time on earth was limited, that it would cheat them all in the end. Before long, these boys would grow old like her. And they, too, would die.

"¿Dónde está la doctora?" Celia flinched at the cold stethoscope on her back and struggled to take a breath.

"She left the country unexpectedly." Dr. Maldonado was curt. "Now cough for me, please." Another round of poking and prodding, a flurry of note-taking on their clacking clipboards, and the lot of them exited at last.

As the island's economy worsened, even the doctors were defecting. Celia had heard of entire families taking to the seas on flimsy rafts, hurricane season or not. Many didn't survive the crossing to Florida and ended up buried at sea. Celia considered her five grandchildren scattered across the globe—in Los Angeles, Miami, Moscow, Berlin—and imagined them waving to her weakly from distant shores. What did she know about any of them?

Celia propped herself on an elbow and considered the photograph of El Líder on the far wall. He was watching over her, como siempre, a cigar jutting from his untamed beard. How virile he was!

Hecho y derecho. His gaze confident, fearless. *Follow me,* it said. This was the same official picture (claro, years out of date) that hung in every hospital room on the island, every post office and provincial town hall, every butcher shop and mechanic's garage, from the illustrious halls of El Capitolio to the shaded Vedado mansion of the Ministry of Culture.

Celia studied El Líder's face and saw a man afraid of being fatally ordinary.

After the triumph of the Revolution, women had shamelessly thrown themselves at El Líder, tossing panties and pañuelos, hoping to detain him on his long march from the Sierra Maestra to Havana. Men all over the island had imitated him and his band of barbudos, germinating scraggly beards that occasioned more abrasions than ardor. But it was El Líder's charisma, his fluency in the language of inspiration, his ability to rally el pueblo, that had kept Celia in his thrall for more than forty years.

Only *he* had never abandoned her. Only *he* had remained steadfast. Only *he* had given her a true sense of purpose. Not like that fickle Gustavo, with his pretty, empty words. Celia looked up at El Líder again, fearing that he might have sensed her fleeting disloyalty.

"I was merely trifling with an extinguished love," she confessed aloud. "Surely you can forgive an old woman's silliness, no?"

Mira, he was smiling at her now, chewing on his Cohiba. Wait. What was he saying? Celia leaned forward, straining to catch his words. His cigar's ribboning smoke encircled her waist, sinuously tugged at her legs. She felt herself rising above the hospital bed, floating toward him, toward his sexy, smoke-expelling mouth. Celia parted her lips to speak but no words came out. Her breathing deepened, became the cloud in which she hovered as the blue smoke turned her like a spit-roasting pig.

She noted with interest the spectacle of her inert body on the hospital bed below, strikingly at odds with her vibrant interior. And what was that spot of blood on her pillow? Had her ear bled from listening for El Líder so intently? Chopin's haunting "Funeral March" filtered through her brain at half tempo. Celia had a soft spot for anything written in the key of B-flat minor. She recalled the Soviet pianist who'd played Rachmaninoff's Piano Sonata no. 2 at the Pro Arte Musical in 1964. Divino el tipo.

"Aguante un poco más, vieja," El Líder insisted. "Que te necesitamos."

Did she detect a note of flirtation in his voice? Ay, it was impossible to refuse this man anything! If he said la revolución still needed her, then it did. If he said her time hadn't come yet, then it hadn't. El Líder lived inside her—a thrilling, galvanizing presence. Sí, she was more tightly bound to him than any lifelong wife could ever be. Celia relaxed her muscles and gradually settled back into her body. El Líder, too, retreated to his portrait and grew still.

To surrender one's life for love, for the loss of it—Celia understood this, having done it twice: first, and recklessly, for Gustavo; second, and more enduringly, for El Líder. But she could no more deny life's inescapable end than believe in an afterlife. The best she could do now was try, for a little longer, to postpone her fate. Celia had no illusions that death would come for her jingling on a bicycle with a rusty bell. No, she suspected, death would arrive like a Stygian owl, all wings and patient majesty, swooping in for the kill.

Herminia Delgado

Santa Teresa del Mar

It was the first Friday in November. As usual, I was visiting Felicia on the outskirts of town. Our little graveyard was nothing fancy, not like the Colón cemetery in Havana, where the island's most decorated generals lay codo a codo with the richest dead. Our cemetery in Santa Teresa del Mar was ill kempt, overgrown with weeds and toppling tombstones. No trimmed hedges, no blooming archways, no graves with fresh-flower wreaths. The best we had were those fat pumpkins on the grave of Fredi Díaz, famous for his green thumb. Nobody dared steal Fredi's calabazas because to steal from the dead was to invite la muerte to your door. And nobody was that hungry— not yet.

A mist shrouded the cemetery, which was as dreary and gray as the tangled net of shadows on Felicia's headstone. The town's only church was nearby, dank and vacant. No priest had said Mass inside those walls for decades. Her epitaph was modest: FELICIA DEL PINO 1938–1980, BELOVED MOTHER, SISTER, DAUGHTER, AND FRIEND. QUE DESCANSE EN PAZ. Nothing that remotely captured her vibrancy, her humor, her outsize generosity for life. We'd been friends from the time we were five and collected seashells together on the beach. Later, we pledged eternal sisterhood with bloody thumbs.

Almost twenty years had passed since her death but I still thought of Felicia every day, visited her every week. Often, we played dominoes on her grave site (she was a ferocious competitor). Or I brought her sprigs of butterfly jasmine from Pinar del Río, where I captured bullfinches and sold them to smugglers for extra money. I built the traps myself and placed them on the forested slopes of the Guaniguanico Mountains. In fact, I had five unhappy birds, caged and waiting, in the backseat of my car.

When Felicia got deathly ill, I took good care of her. I fed and bathed her, briefed her on the latest gossip, refreshed her tureen of sacred stones. Like me, she was a santera. Our rituals were healing, but in the end, nothing could save her. La pobre looked a lot happier dead than alive—everyone in the casa de santos said so. The lumps on her head disappeared, her skin became conch-smooth, and her hands were as plumply dimpled as a baby's.

Our religious elders carefully anointed Felicia's body for burial and prepared morsels of smoked fish and corn for her journey. During the funeral procession, her old 1952 DeSoto broke down—the same car she'd bequeathed to me, its paint peeling, its upholstery blistered by the sun. That malhumorado cacharro still got me around most days. And when its radio sputtered to life, I listened to reruns of the Wolfman Jack show beamed in from Key West. Ay, that Wolfman's voice was puro guarapo! It stirred me like when I was a teenager y enamorándome left and right.

Each time I visited Felicia at the cemetery I offered prayers for my son, too, though he wasn't buried there. How could he be, when his body was blown apart on a savanna in Angola? It was all I could do not to slap people who insisted that my Joaquín was a hero of the Revolution. What business did Cuba have sending its boys to die in a war thousands of miles from home? For years I was haunted by the thought of his terror as the land mine tore him apart. Did he even have time to say a last prayer?

In the spring my younger son, Eusebio, was branded a traitor for escaping the island on a balsa he'd built himself. Neighbors blamed me for what happened. They shunned me, questioned my loyalty to la revolución. Eusebio had been a Young Pioneer, on the national gymnastics team, volunteered for everything under the sun. His hands were callused from countless zafras. Who bothered to remember any of that? But once-devout revolutionaries also grew tired of sacrificing their lives with nothing to show for it.

The way I saw it, nobody expected the Revolution to come to ruins. For all the talk of independence, our island simply exchanged one dependency for another. We thought we were building something extraordinary, a model for other developing nations fighting imperialism. Créame, we learned our lesson the hardest way possible. When the Soviet Union fell apart, the last thing on their minds was: *What will happen to Cuba?*

Now, I wasn't one to go singing the praises of the USSR, but at least they provided us with basic stability and a few imports: toothpaste and TV sets, canned plums, even those junky Ladas that our mechanics miraculously kept running. Jokingly, we called the Russians "bolos," or bowling pins (you could imagine why), but at least they were predictable. We paid a high price for that predictability.

Me? I was close to retiring when the government shut down the battery factory where I'd worked for thirty-two years. No pensions, nada. From one day to the next, eighty-six people were out of a job, including two rusas—Niurka and Ludmila—who'd come to Cuba in the seventies. Their exchange-student husbands had promised them that they'd live like queens here. But those Russian girls ended up suffering, just like us.

Sometimes when I visited Felicia, she whispered her concerns to me from the beyond. Her biggest worry was her son, Ivanito, who lived far away in Berlin, doing who knew what. Felicia also lamented her choice of husbands—one worse than the next, if you asked me. The truth was that a woman's regrets were eternal. But that first Friday in November she was unusually quiet. I tried tempting her with the latest indiscretions by our fourth-generation Lothario postman. Pero nada.

"Where've you gone, Felicia? Are you traveling?"

No response.

I guessed she was feeling moody about something or other. Felicia tended to withdraw when she was brooding, or depressed. I kept having to remind myself that she was dead. Felicia used to dream of visiting La Virgen de la Caridad at her cathedral in El Cobre *before she ran out of miracles*. Imagínate, as if La Virgen had only a finite number of them!

"Mira, I brought you butterfly jasmine." I held up some for her to see.

Silence.

"Ay, you know how much I hate talking to myself!" I wasn't one for monologues, or speechifying, like so many bambolleros on the island, beginning with *you know who*.

More silence.

"I have big news, chica, but you can't tell a soul!"

Out of nowhere a land crab ambled across her grave. Perhaps Felicia had sent it my way as a consolation gift? I scooped it up and slipped it into my bag. Luckily, I'd just fixed the zipper, so no way el cangrejo could escape. It would make a tasty dinner.

"Next week's your birthday! Sixty-one! We got older than old, eh?" I squatted at the foot of Felicia's grave, my knees popping. "Bueno, querida, I'll be back next week, como siempre. Adiós por ahora."

As I turned to leave, a bullfinch landed on Felicia's tombstone—a male in full plumage, its underwings starched white, like innocence itself. It stared at me, then lifted its head and began singing a todo meter. My first impulse was to capture it with my pañuelo and take it home with the other birds. It would fetch a nice price, well above average. His beak widened and trembled as he sang, his little body bursting with conviction.

It seemed that he was trying to tell me something important, as if insisting: *Your days are so few, Herminia! What are you doing with your life?*

BERLIN-MOSCOW

I

~ ◦ ~

Ivanito Villaverde

Berlin

It was weeks before Ivanito saw his mother again, this time in a
cracked mirror at the gay bathhouse off Nollendorfplatz. He was
naked except for his spiked cuffs, matching dog collar, and black
leather boots slung with chains, its toes metal-tipped. Nobody recognized him here, and he liked it that way. Here he was simply
another pretty boy—a choice bit of anonymous bottom—tall and
delicate-boned, with shoulder-length hair and small, inviting ears.

As his mother hovered in the mirror, she seemed oblivious to
the surroundings, taking no notice of the trio of men cavorting
nearby, the burliest with a medieval scabbard tattooed down his
spine. Mami's face serenely bobbed atop a kaleidoscopic haze of
pastels. She reminded Ivanito of a documentary he'd once seen
on squids. Then she oozed out of the mirror and grinned at him,
her gums an unnatural pink. The color disturbed Ivanito but he
refrained from overreacting. He wanted to keep her present long
enough to find out why she'd returned from the dead.

Ivanito signaled for his mother to wait for him as he changed
into his street clothes, bundling up in a down jacket and fashionable
rabbit-fur hat. Then he beckoned Mami to follow him out into frigid,
predawn Berlin. Together they hurried down Fuggerstrasse, past
linden trees thinly sheathed with frost. On the opposite sidewalk

a disheveled woman strode lopsidedly, one bare foot in the gutter, the other on the curb.

"Are you hungry, Mami? Do ghosts even get hungry?"

"Bratwurst . . ."

Ivanito was taken aback. His mother was nearly twenty years dead, and this was her first word—and uttered with a perfect German accent? But it so happened that bratwurst was exactly what he wanted, too. Could Mami read his mind, as he'd believed as a boy? And when the hell had she learned German? Did people spontaneously become multilingual at death?

He led his mother to a popular, twenty-four-hour Schnellimbiss and they got in line behind the city's haggard demimonde, who were stamping their feet to stay warm. Nobody seemed to notice her at all. Was she invisible to everyone but him?

Ivanito ordered three bratwursts and offered one to his mother. Mami absorbed it all—sausage, roll, spicy mustard—into her billowing mists and issued a demure burp. Impressive, he thought, devouring his first bratwurst, then attacking the second. His hands were greasy from the mess. His mother declined a napkin.

"¿Quieres más?" he asked.

"Home." Mami's voice was barely audible.

Home? Ivanito was unnerved. What did she mean by "home"? Home to his Charlottenburg apartment, less than a mile away? Home to their tumbledown house back on Palmas Street? Or was home with his mother, in the realm of the dead?

Overhead a flock of greylag geese was flying south—mysteriously, in winter (they should have left a month ago). Ivanito broke into a run until he, too, felt like he was flying. Mami sailed beside him as he pumped his arms, his feet barely touching the ground, the cold air freezing his lungs. She laughed as they ran, like she used to when they'd raced through Havana's parks chasing pigeons and dreams, or so she'd claimed.

His mother effortlessly floated up the four flights of stairs to his

apartment, and Ivanito ushered her in. A vase of dying gladioli suf-
fused the rooms with a rotting scent. Mami settled, undulating, on
the living room sofa and took a look around. She gaped like a tourist at the shelves crowded with books, the Bauhaus furniture, his
eclectic collection of antiques. Ivanito put Mozart's Violin Concerto
no. 3 on the turntable—to calm himself, and gauge her response.
She began awkwardly swaying to the music, as if it were danceable.

In another life Ivanito might have become a classical musician,
played the violin's dangerous nerve endings. Instead he became a
translator, fluent in Spanish, Russian, English, and German. Ivanito
translated these languages but also their cultures, their histories,
their erotics, their losses, shape-shifting from one lexicon to the
next.

"Por favor, Mami," he said softly. "Can you stay awhile? I have a
million questions." Ivanito poured her a generous tumbler of rum
and another one for himself. She belted hers back without ceremony,
then held up her glass for a refill. ¿Y por qué no? Things couldn't
be stranger, yet they felt oddly familiar to him. What would it take
to tip him to insanity?

"Mi cielo." His mother's voice was gentle, at its most maternal.
She leaned toward him and Ivanito surrendered to the lost pleasure
of her embrace. A soporific heat seeped through his scalp, lulling
him to sleep. When he opened his eyes an hour later, Mami was
gone. Ivanito forced himself not to cry. How many times could she
abandon him in one lifetime?

Years ago his mother had been laid to rest in a white gown and
turban and draped with elekes, religious beads. As santería priests
played the holy batá drums, pallbearers carried her coffin to the
cemetery outside Santa Teresa del Mar. Everyone seemed to forget
that Ivanito was there, lost and grieving in his ill-fitting funeral suit.
He had planned to drop a gift into Mami's grave—a duckling he'd
stolen—but the duckling had died, too.

From his locked desk drawer, Ivanito extracted the diary his mother had left him. Plum-colored, with fading gold stars, it was the only thing of hers he owned. He flipped through the blank yellowed pages. She'd kept it in the false bottom of her hairdresser's tool kit—beneath the pink plastic curlers and the hair dryer that blew out the electricity in his grandmother's seaside house. Ivanito had taken this diary everywhere—on the long journey to New York, then to Moscow, and, finally, to Berlin.

It occurred to him that terror inhabited Mami's diary, the terror of erasure. Had she hoped that he might fill these pages with his own history? Write over the invisible palimpsest of her own? Or perhaps she'd longed for their voices to merge, to grow louder and more insistent together? But he never wrote a word. After her death, Ivanito often defended his mother against those who'd accused her of feigning madness, defying the Revolution, and, worst of all, attempting to kill him when he was five.

The skies were cloudy, devoid of stars. Only the streetlamps blazed along the empty, frozen boulevards of Berlin. Ivanito was as exhausted as he'd ever felt. As he prepared for bed, he caught a glimpse of himself in the dim light of the closet door mirror. There, glowing softly around his head, was a halo.

2

Irina del Pino

Moscow

Irina del Pino struggled to walk in the opposite direction of a massive demonstration on Tsverskaya Street, the crowd thick with nostalgia and the stink of vodka. It was a cold November afternoon, the sky feathered in pearly grays. She shuddered as the sea of protesters croaked out the depressing old national anthem.

> *United forever in friendship and labor,*
> *Our mighty republics will ever endure,*
> *The Great Soviet Union will live through the ages.*
> *The dream of a people, their fortress secure . . .*

The fanfare was reminiscent of Soviet-era parades, with their red seas of flags and banners emblazoned with the hammer and sickle. Today, the marchers carried portraits of Lenin and Stalin adorned with crepe paper (unthinkable just a few years ago), alongside posters of Brezhnev lacquered in medals. Many shook signs with anti-capitalist slogans: GORBACHEV STOLE MY MOTHERLAND! DOWN WITH KGB CAPITALISTS! RUSSIA IS NOT FOR SALE! There was a blown-up photo of a cigar-smoking Fidel Castro in fatigues and a vendor selling Che Guevara buttons for ten rubles.

Irina wasn't unsympathetic to the protesters but she considered herself more of a pragmatist, a Realpolitiker. This was uncommon in Moscow, where she'd been raised by her Czech mother and Russian stepfather. She'd come a long way from her upbringing, in a bleak communal apartment housing thirteen people. Why would she want to turn the clock back to Soviet times? To what? The string bags of raw chicken hanging from their balcony? The bleach-and-rags smell of her school cafeteria? Their drunk neighbor passed out with pissed-in pants down the hall? Nyet, spasiba.

The country had fallen to pieces faster than anyone could've anticipated, careening from a sputtering black-and-white Soviet film into a capitalist one bursting with color and chaos. Under Communism even minor extravagances were considered "unacceptable exclusivity." Yet overnight, Russia was overrun with billboards and shiny offerings from the West: televisions, kitchen appliances, luxury German cars, Mediterranean citrus. Irina's first purchase after the Soviet Union went belly-up? A pineapple. It was delicious.

Soon after the collapse, Irina dropped out of college—and abandoned a promising career as a statistician—to privatize Uplift, a state-owned brassiere factory, with Mafia-financed vouchers. Apocalypse or not, women still needed bras. And better than the old Soviet ones, which, with their pointed cups and ungainly armature, repelled all but the most determined suitors. The factory workers at Uplift mistrusted Irina at first, eyeing her up and down, as if to say: *Who do you think you are, little girl?* But steady paychecks were a rarity then, and all 177 of them stayed.

Irina worked tirelessly to update the factory's production lines and secured a hard-currency authorization to import luxury fabrics. In its first season, the newly renamed Caress produced sexy, soft-cupped bras in a dozen styles and colors. By its third year in operation, the company earned an unprecedented thirty-seven-percent profit after rolling out its "Sputnik" line of retro lingerie: shimmery crimson-and-silver corsets, negligees, push-up bras, garter belts, and crotchless panties, all of which proved wildly popular in the former Soviet bloc.

The marchers lurched toward Red Square, bellicose with griev-ances. "Our country needs freedom like a monkey needs glasses!" shouted a skeletal man with taped-together spectacles. "They flushed our country down the toilet!" This from a one-legged veteran fes-tooned with war medals from Afghanistan. "Russia needs a strong hand, an overseer with a stick!" a toothless man muttered, clinging to his bottle of Stolichnaya.

There was no denying their misery. Russian society was starkly divided in two—those with money, and those without. Irina was definitely on the monied side. Not oligarchic money, but money just the same. It had become her definition of freedom. This was an ongoing argument with her stepfather, a mathematician–turned–Marxist philosophy professor. After losing his university position, he turned to selling Soviet memorabilia to "parasite tourists"—his phrase—on the Arbat. "Get your authentic totalitarian relics here!" Despondent, he subsisted on vodka and loans from Irina.

Two years ago, when she handed off her last cash payment to the mobsters who'd bankrolled her factory, Irina wore a bulletproof vest and had a Tokarev tucked inside the holster of her thigh-high boot. (By then she was proficient with multiple firearms, including Makarovs and Kalashnikovs.) As for the rest, what could she do? Despite its many crises, Russia was home—and as expansive as her ambition. She couldn't imagine living in just any little mousetrap of a country, though her cultural origins hadn't promised much of a future.

Irina's chauffeur was waiting on a side street, as prearranged. She slid into the backseat of her Mercedes E-55 sedan, poured herself a glass of chilled Shuiskaya, and nursed it in the miserable traffic home. It was Friday, and Irina was worn out. She'd been wrangling for days with her operations manager—the theatrically stubborn

Galina Budnikova—over reconfiguring the last decrepit production lines. Irina had never dreamed of being the brassiere queen of Russia. Yet that was precisely who she'd become.

Despite her hard-won success, Irina was alone in the world. Her parents were dead—her Czech mother from a morphine overdose six years ago; her biological Cuban father by suicide when she was a little girl. Sometimes when Irina drank too much—on weekends, mostly—she studied the sole photograph she had of Javier del Pino, cradling her as a newborn. How elated her father looked, as if he couldn't believe that this tiny slip of a girl was his. Her parents had met as doctoral students in chemistry at the University of Prague in the summer of 1968. Hopes had been impossibly high then—for democracy, for freedom, even for love.

Irina unlocked the front door of her penthouse on Ostozhenka Street. Her living room windows overlooked the Moscow River, where a handful of mallards lingered. The golden domes of the Kadashi, once an Orthodox church, merged with the dusk. She considered her greatest luxury to be living alone. At home, all was calm predictability. Her Austrian chef had prepared a gourmet meal worthy of the Hapsburgs: liver pâté with black truffles, sautéed breast of pheasant and wild mushrooms, a Sacher torte with fresh whipped cream for dessert.

After dinner Irina cracked open a window and inhaled the desiccated scents of late autumn. Then she lit a cigarette and watched an American movie on her satellite TV. It was about a Black lounge singer who was hiding from gangsters in a Catholic convent in San Francisco. Irina enjoyed the film—such exuberant singing!—but she was perplexed by the concept of the U.S. witness protection program. As far back as the czar's day, witnesses testified what they'd been instructed to say, nothing more. Every case was decided ahead of time. It wasn't justice but it was expedient.

Irina poured herself a double shot of Havana Club 7 and nestled under her Siberian snow-goose-down comforter. The aged rum warmed her chest, and she topped off her glass twice. What was Cuba to her now except a crocodile-shaped island on a vanishing map, foreign and far away? Was there anyone left there she could call family? Who would remember her father, Javier del Pino? Or that his daughter existed half a world away?

Irina's mother had told her stories about the good-looking exchange student from Havana whom she'd impulsively married after only a few weeks. How Javier had taught her how to rumba, which naturally led to . . . *Why are you so curious, Irina? You're much too young for this story!* Her parents married eight days before a half-million Soviet troops crushed the Czechs' brief flirtation with change. Irina tried to imagine Maminka madly in love, not the hollow-eyed nurse she later became, wasting away her final years.

Except for her paleness, Irina bore a striking resemblance to her father. She'd inherited his angular face, his muscular lankiness, his large-knuckled hands and size-ten feet. All of which had come in handy for her as a fencer (she'd competed regionally as a teenager). The few French words she knew—*Allez! Battez! En garde!*—were from the sport. Occasionally, Irina cultivated her likeness to Javier del Pino by gluing on a strip of mustache, slicking back her hair with a glossy pomade, and donning a Panama hat. It was not beyond her to seduce a lingerie model from time to time, chalking it up to research.

Early next spring, Irina planned to open a factory in Berlin with a consortium of European investors. She would be launching a line of fashionable sportswear for customers who hated exercise but wanted to look athletic. No matter how out of shape women got, they remained transfixed by the image of themselves at nineteen. Irina's sportwear, with its hidden girders and strategic spandex, ensured that they approached their ideals. To appear fit, after all, was the new status symbol.

Irina turned off the lights and lay smoking in the dark. She had no religion except for a staunch belief in the future, which had proved more consistently reliable than the past. It soothed her to plan ahead, to prepare for the unexpected. The world she'd grown up with had disappeared nearly a decade ago, but she'd seized her opportunity—*snap*, like the jaws of a Kamchatka bear—and had been reaping the benefits ever since.

3

Ivanito Villaverde

Berlin

Ivanito suspected that his mother was transmitting a steady stream of subliminal messages through the halo into his brain. He knew how crazy that sounded, which was why he hadn't told a soul. The halo was getting heavier, too, more unwieldy, like a growing rack of antlers, and its bottom edge was singeing his skull. Ivanito checked his feverish scalp for blistering, but the skin remained smooth. He hadn't seen Mami in over a month, as if she were biding her time until her control over him was complete.

Was he losing his mind? Ivanito had made numerous appointments with psychologists only to promptly cancel them. Since he alone could see the halo—and hear its intermittent pinging, like soft hammer blows against the burnished gold—they would likely diagnose him as schizophrenic. Next stop? Some mental health facility in a leafy suburb of Berlin. Did he really need to invite more trouble into his life?

It was four in the morning, and Ivanito stirred from another wretched night's sleep. As always, he was lonely for Sergei Volchkov, the Bolshoi dancer whom Ivanito had first seen perform Von Roth-bart in *Swan Lake* on a hazy spring night in Moscow. Sergei's turns were heart-stopping, his jumps defied time, and he was gorgeous enough to have been sculpted by Pheidias. After the show, Ivanito bribed his way backstage to meet him.

What followed was a romance worthy of Tolstoy—or so he'd thought.

Sergei had grown up in St. Petersburg near the Neva River, and Pushkin's monument, and Gogol's inimitable tales. He'd lived with his babushka, a snuff-snorting survivor of the Nazi blockade and an ardent Tolstoy fan. "You sound like Count Vronsky himself!" she laughed, teasing Ivanito about his formal Russian. On that same visit to St. Petersburg, Sergei confessed that he'd begun fucking someone in the corps de ballet. A woman, a ballerina. Someone Ivanito could never be.

A breeze rustled the chestnut tree outside his window. The streets were deserted. Ivanito unclenched his fists, which were tense enough to throw a punch. He'd never felt so prone to violence. He lit a cigarette and scanned his apartment for minor disturbances: sugar bowl overturned, lights left on, egg cups cracked or gone missing, the dwindling supply of rum. Who else could he blame but his dead mother?

The subtle scent of gardenias cut through the unfurling cigarette smoke. Ivanito's chest tightened. Had he conjured her with his suspicions?

"You don't feel the cold?" Mami's voice boomed out from the oval mirror above his Biedermeier dresser. She was minuscule this time, like a photograph in an old-fashioned locket, her face much younger-looking and focused on him.

"De vez en cuando." Ivanito spoke slowly, afraid that she might disappear. Or worse, that he'd realize she wasn't there at all.

"You must feel it now."

"I do." Only the smoke's warmth kept the chill at bay, though he didn't say this. In Cuba his mother had felt cold on the hottest July days.

"Can I have one?" she asked, shivering.

Ivanito tapped a cigarette out of his pack of Camels. It automatically adjusted to Mami's size as she slipped the cigarette between her diminutive lips. He flicked on his nickel-plated Sputnik lighter, which looked like a bonfire approaching her. Before he could bring the flame any closer, his mother's cigarette lit itself.

Nice trick, he wanted to say, but didn't. Better to watch, and wait.

"I think I'm catching a cold." She sniffled for emphasis.

"Is that possible where you are?" Ivanito smiled in spite of himself. Mami's self-absorption could be endearing sometimes. Her face was smaller than a plum, bigger than a grape. Was it her size that was making him feel generous toward her?

"What do you mean *where you are*? I'm with you. Freezing in Berlin."

"Winters can be brutal. Everyone knows that."

"It's a city of ice. People sleep on their hearts here."

Was that barb aimed at him? Ivanito often lulled himself to sleep by resting a hand on his chest, like a baby soothed by his mother's heartbeat.

"How can you stay here?" Her breathing sounded laborious.

"It's where I'm living my life."

"But you're a tropical boy."

"Not anymore."

To his surprise, Mami pulled a tiny carrot from a hidden pocket and bit into it.

"Are you a health nut now?"

"I'm giving it a try." She took another desultory bite.

"When I die, I'll eat nothing but cream puffs."

Mami laughed, choking on the carrot. "That could be arranged, mijo."

"Don't get too excited. I'm not ready to go yet."

His mother grew serious. Tiny blue flames were whipping around her temples like hummingbirds. Was he imagining this?

"I see you, mijo."

"I see you, too, Mami."

"I drift into your dreams at night."

"I don't have dreams." This wasn't true but Ivanito refused to indulge her grandiosity.

"Through the halo. Didn't you know?"

"I suspected as much." Ivanito took a last drag of his cigarette, then dropped it into the mug of cold tea on his nightstand.

"I dream without the bother of sleep. It's one of the perks of being dead." His mother discarded the wisp of carrot top and continued smoking. Her cigarette looked newly lit. Had it become infinite, like her?

"You're resisting me." Mami's voice was flat. "For the first time, mi cielo."

Ivanito sensed the turbulence beneath her outward calm. "Yes, I believe I am." He avoided looking at her directly, fixating instead on the Trabert table lamp he'd bought for a song at an antiques shop on Suarezstrasse.

"But why? You'll ruin everything!" Mami's face inflated with momentary emotion before contracting back to cameo size. "Aren't you still my boy? My sweet, loyal boy?"

Why did his mother believe she was forever entitled to his loyalty, no matter how badly she behaved? She was acting as if her death were an injustice, an unwarranted exile, and that he was somehow to blame. They stared at each other until Ivanito felt like a clay figure connected to her by threads of dust. At Mami's burial, a swirl of wind had whisked away the first clod of earth meant to secure her belowground. Then her mouth flung open and nobody could close it again. His mother was buried like that—mouth agape, molars missing, gums visible.

"We belong together, mijo," Mami said finally. "You'll only rest when you're . . ." Her voice trailed off.

"When I'm what?" he demanded, arms stiff at his sides.

"Love is made up of sacrifices." Her cigarette dangled indecorously from her lips.

The halo felt like an icy garland around his head. Was it presaging his martyrdom? Ivanito tried to fathom which version of impossible might come next. So, eternity had a voice and it sounded like his mother? Increíble.

"Who are you, really?" he asked, startling them both.

"Always and only, your mother." Then she sighed imperiously and, arching an eyebrow, disappeared into the recesses of the mirror.

Mami was a natural diva. How well she understood the principles of enthralling an audience, timing an exit, leaving her fans begging for more. These lessons had served Ivanito onstage. But recognizing the artifice didn't stop the familiar surge of loss in his chest.

LOS ANGELES-MIAMI

I

Pilar Puente

Los Angeles

It was the cusp of winter, mild and fragrant with lilac verbena. The sky was striated with fuchsias and maroons and shot through with neon tangerines. The pollution was oppressive in Los Angeles but it offered up spectacular sunsets. Cascades of bougainvillea framed my living room windows. The blossoms grew dark with dusk, smudging the whitewashed walls. A hummingbird angled over the jasmine.

I was lucky enough to live in Santa Monica Canyon in a ramshackle rental house overlooking the ocean. Every day—like Abuela Celia in Cuba—I peered through binoculars out to sea, though the Pacific's slate-gray waves had nothing on the Caribbean's blues. From here I spotted dolphins frolicking along the coast; twice I'd seen migrating whales. Seabirds performed in a continual aerial circus. During the winter rains, my ceilings leaked constantly. Downpours sounded like a madness of castanets.

Six years ago I became a mother. This raising of a boy, a baby man, was scrambling my relationship to gender and showing up in my sculptures (the few I was doing) in unexpected ways. For a group show last year, I created an androgynous homunculus with sound-sensitive eyes. It responded to birdsong—Cuban bullfinches, in particular—which a tropical ornithologist identified at the opening.

The *L.A. Weekly* praised the piece: "A postcolonial commentary on the imperium of the sensorial."

Whatever. It still didn't get me a tenure-track job anywhere.

The fact was that motherhood was a wrecking ball with no warning label, wreaking havoc on my body, soul, dreams, moods, focus, sleep, and artistic life. Not an option for most of the female sculptors I knew. Azul wasn't difficult, just relentlessly there. I felt crushed by the ongoing burden of it all, by my lack of solitude, by my persistent doughiness. Mostly I sat staring, vacant-eyed, inside my moldy backyard studio and wondering how my life had gotten to this point. Was it too much to want significance?

Male artists always found women to take care of their children. My own son's father was a case in point. He'd made it abundantly clear that my pregnancy would have zero bearing on his personal or professional plans. Haru Tanaka was married and fifteen years older than me. He was renowned for his Wunderkammer—provocative, warehouse-size affairs—that evoked Imperial Japan. With his anachronistic English, Haru was not beyond issuing devastating judgments. Once, he called me (and by extension, my work) an "epigone," as if I were an unoriginal, foregone conclusion.

We were in love, or so I'd believed, but Haru kept his word. I was alone when I gave birth to Azul—and I'm still alone. Haru took more than my heart when he left. Why had I let him shatter me?

My son was fearsomely articulate—and, like most six-year-olds, had nothing but time on his hands. That made everything negotiable: junk food, teeth-brushing, radio stations. Last week he put his tiny fists on his hips and sniped: "Who made you the boss of me, anyway?" Nature versus nurture? Were you fucking kidding me? And, I'd learned, he could dismember any doll in thirty seconds flat.

"Good for him!" Mom crowed when I told her about it. "My boy won't let you turn him into a mariconcito like all your artist friends!"

Azul was my mother's principal reason for living. She was interested only in what *her boy* was doing. Teething, toilet-training, kindergarten, a penchant for wasabi peas—everything was endlessly fascinating to her. My life, beyond being the humble vehicle from which this miracle child had emerged, was of scant importance. I pretended not to care, but the resentments kept piling up. My sole power? Withholding her precious grandson for months at a time. It gave me a keen understanding of the dynamics of emotional ransom.

The art scene in Los Angeles was on fire, the equivalent of Seattle just after Nirvana's *Nevermind* went platinum. But I wasn't part of the gold rush. Aside from my meager productivity, I'd been sidelined for being too difficult, like some spoiled Hollywood starlet. "You're unwilling to cultivate collectors," my ex-gallerist told me, meaning I refused to kiss ass, to switch on for them like a goddamn lightbulb. "Are we artists, or public relations shills?" I shouted at him before storming off.

If punk had taught me anything, it was to take no prisoners—just like that old Lou Reed album—to be bold, unapologetic. I missed those days hanging out on the Lower East Side with my cousin Ivanito. For a few years we'd been each other's inseparable sidekicks. Our band, Autopsy, had its flash of glory in 1984, thanks to him. I played bass and wrote the lyrics but Ivanito sang his heart out center stage. Our one club hit, "Litterbox Heart," took the downtown punk scene by storm.

It was getting late but I put on *¡Adios Amigos!*, the last recorded album by the Ramones. For the final song, "Born to Die in Berlin," I plugged in my amp and lugged my bass out of the closet. I held it really low, letting the pickup sit right on my pubic bone. Damn, if its raw sexual energy didn't go right through me.

Sometimes I feelin' that my soul is as restless as the wind
Maybe I was born to die in Berlin . . .

2

Lourdes Puente

Miami

A boy, it was always a boy at the core of Lourdes Puente's heart-aches. The unborn son whom she would have named Jorgito, after her father. Her nephew, Ivanito, who'd broken her heart by taking off to study in Russia, of all places. And now her only grandson was living in Los Angeles without a father to keep an eye on him, to combat the confusions about masculinity that ran rampant in Pilar's artistic circles.

Not to mention the abnormal dietary restrictions imposed on him. If her daughter chose to be a vegetarian, who cared? But Azu-lito wouldn't grow another inch without meat! How could Pilar refuse her own son the taste of lechón asado? Or the juicy heft of a medianoche (pickles were vegetables, no?). She'd declared war on sugar, too. ¡Azúcar! Not Communism, ¡qué va! That would be too easy. Sugar was the enemy now. Why, she was positively anti-Cuban!

Recently, Lourdes had grown fixated on the tragic case of Eliseo González—the boy found clinging to an inner tube in the Straits of Florida on Thanksgiving Day. His mother and everyone traveling with them had drowned trying to escape Cuba. Such a beautiful boy, too, sweet-faced and shy, and with an extraordinary will to live! Little Eliseo would grow up to do great things—of that Lourdes was certain. She tried to talk to her husband about the boy's plight, but Rufino, who was studying for his boat captain's license, paid her no mind.

If only she could get to know Eliseo better, treat him to a cheeseburger, things Lourdes couldn't do with her own grandson. Perhaps she might offer to take him to Disney World? Or pay for a year's tuition at a Catholic school so that the nuns, por lo menos, could drum any vestigial Communism out of him. Eliseo's father—a lowly hotel waiter in Cárdenas—was intent on hauling the boy back to the island with El Líder's help. ¡Qué barbaridad!

Lourdes called her daughter to discuss an urgent matter regarding the Eliseo case—namely, the public relations disaster that was his teenage cousin Marisol, who shot off her mouth to anyone with a microphone. That vulgar girl was making the whole exile community look bad. At minimum, the González family should hire a spokesperson who would better represent the more sophisticated cubanos in Miami.

"You're a snob," Pilar said. "And ridiculous."

"You have the nerve to call me ridiculous?" Lourdes snapped. "What about that Statue of Liberty you painted for my bakery? With a maldito safety pin through her nose? Ridiculous *and* disrespectful!"

"You just always think you're right."

"I think, therefore I am."

"You don't even know who Descartes is!"

"De quién?"

"I rest my case. I have to go now."

It was utterly useless. She and Pilar couldn't be more on the opposite sides of everything. It was her fate, Lourdes thought sadly, to be trapped between a Communist mother and a hippie daughter aligned against her.

"Are you coming to Miami for Christmas?" Lourdes rushed to ask before Pilar hung up.

"Not happening."

Lourdes drove to the twenty-four-hour chapel on Key Biscayne to simmer down. She lit five votive candles, though she paid for only one. The candles were overpriced and she refused to be gouged, least of all in church. Lourdes knelt before the alcove of La Virgen de la Caridad del Cobre, inhaling the frankincense from an earlier Mass. On her twelfth Hail Mary, Lourdes heard a voice—female, ethereal, not her own, and yet a part of her.

You will save the boy found at sea.

She gazed up at La Virgen, whose lips were moving slightly. Lourdes dropped her rosary, which scuttled under the padded kneeler like a scorpion. Only the rosary's crucifix peeked out from the wood, glinting with stained-glass light.

For the son you lost. For all our precious boys lost to war. This is your mission.

Lourdes crossed herself three times, hands shaking. Was La Virgen really choosing *her*?

She hurried home and changed into her knitted navy-blue St. John suit. It made her feel invincible, like her auxiliary-policewoman uniform in Brooklyn used to do. Then she draped a patriotic silk scarf over her shoulders. By the time Lourdes got behind the wheel of her lavender Jaguar, her chest was swelling with purpose. The engine was quiet, the air-conditioning preset to fifty-eight degrees, the radio tuned to Radio Mambí, the most anti-Communist of the local stations.

As she drove along Cranston Boulevard, a flash of rain gave Key Biscayne an otherworldly air. Portents were everywhere. A bicyclist flashed her a victory sign for no apparent reason. A formation of seagulls spelled out her name—minus the s—in the northern skies. And she cruised right through every green light on her way off the island. When did that ever happen?

Lourdes's confidence grew as she crossed the Rickenbacker Causeway. The skyline of Brickell Avenue loomed with promise, fortifying her sense of righteousness. The radio was playing Olga Guillot's

"La Gloria Eres Tú" and Lourdes joined in at the top of her lungs. She was heading straight to Little Havana, to the modest white bungalow where Eliseo lived. As she slipped onto one highway, then another, Lourdes felt a divine light sweeping through her, guiding her toward her destiny.

INTERLUDE: PILAR'S PHOTOS

Image #1: 1961

It's the moment we leave Cuba. My mother is dressed like a steward-ess, sleek in her two-piece suit. It's a black-and-white photo but the suit looks navy blue, her favorite color. Mom is wearing high heels and false eyelashes for the forty-five-minute flight. Her hair is arranged in a stylish twist, topped with a pert pillbox hat. She hasn't seen my father in six months—he went ahead to Miami before sending for us—and she's anxious to look beautiful, better than he remembers. It's difficult to reconcile this glamorous, wasp-waisted woman with the one in a size-twenty-six bakery uniform, sporting a hairnet and orthopedic shoes, and gobbling up pecan sticky buns by the truckload.

It's the end of March, and I'm two years and three months old. Mom holds my hand but the tilt of my body shows that I'm pulling away from her—if not pulling, exactly, then leaning hard in the opposite direction. This gesture—how early it appears—captures our lifelong interactions. How do I already know to keep a safe distance from her? Am I rebelling against the scratchy organza-and-crinoline party dress? My shiny patent-leather shoes? To this day, Mom accuses me of being unsociable and indifferent to my appear-ance. The antithesis of a true cubana. As if my sloppy ponytail and corduroys were direct assaults on her femininity.

In the photo we're standing next to an American Airlines propeller plane—an old puddle jumper—that will fly us from Havana to Miami, though the distance we'll travel is farther than either of us can imagine. Dad will be waiting with orchids for Mom, a stuffed pink rabbit for me. As my toddler self searches for an exit, my mouth is compressed into tight refusal. I'm tempted to caption myself: *Hell no, I won't go!* Who took this picture, anyway? I'm guessing it was another passenger, or maybe the pilot on his way to the cockpit. Mom has never been shy about ordering total strangers around.

What I remember most clearly is what happened the day before, when I was sitting in Abuela Celia's lap and playing with her drop-pearl earrings. We were in the wicker swing on her porch, overlooking the sea. The sun was high and the air smelled sweet from the jasmine and gardenia trees. Waves gently lapped the shore. The squeaking swing kept time with the lullaby my grandmother sang to me: *Duérmete mi niña / duérmete mi amor / duérmete pedazo / de mi corazón . . .*

I'd been staying with Abuela Celia while my mother finished preparations for our departure to Miami. But I didn't want to go. I felt most at home in my grandmother's lap. *Leave her with me,* she told Mom. *You have many hardships ahead, mija. I'll take care of Pilar until you're ready.* But my mother yelled at her, called El Líder a butcher. I remember the word *butcher* because it made me wonder what we were having for lunch. Pork chops, I hoped, with crispy tostones. *She'll be safe here. Por favor, Lourdes.*

There was more shouting, a scuffle. I clung to my grandmother, buried my face in her talcumed neck. Then Mom yanked me out of Abuela Celia's arms. *Nooooooooooo!*

Image #2: 1964

I'm five years old and standing next to my father at Sunken Meadow Beach on Long Island. I don't yet know the word *paradox,* about how a meadow might sink and become a stretch of sand seducing the sea. But I was intrigued by the name all the same. In the photo I'm wearing a red, white, and blue two-piece bathing suit with a ruffled bottom (Mom was partial to patriotic attire even then). Baby fat spills over my waistband. My hair is in a pixie cut and I'm looking up at my dad, who's grinning, his hand casually resting on my shoulder.

I can't take my eyes off him.

Dad is movie-star handsome. And his hair! There's just so much of it, a halo of inky blackness. I barely recognize him. He looks relaxed, too. Not paunchy or grouchy, not trapped inside our Brooklyn warehouse with his useless inventions. His swimming trunks are baggy and sport two shiny snaps at the waist. I realize now that I don't know my father at all, the man he was before Mom twisted him into someone else. The man who once confided in me that he would flee to Africa if he could, far from his failures in New York. Is it any wonder he sought other ways to feel worthy?

My sunburnt arms hang awkwardly, as if they're new appendages that I'm still learning how to use. I detect a hint of confusion in my expression. Who knows what Mom is saying as she takes the picture? My smile looks semi-forced. Admittedly this is a retroactive perspective but I'm not that different now, just more articulate.

The beach is crowded. It's probably August. It takes that long for the Atlantic to warm up enough to go swimming. Nowadays I only swim in Caribbean-temperature waters. This may be the one certifiable way I'm Cuban. In the picture, Dad and I are a stone's throw from the surf. A lumpish woman behind us adjusts her floral bathing cap, the kind that cuts off circulation to the face. Clumps of families wade into the sea, feast on picnics (are those sausage heroes?), toss beach balls. A toddler mimics her mother by placing her hands on her hips.

Was there ever a time when I, too, mimicked my mother? Wanted to grow up and be like her? When I revolved around her like a tiny planet beholden to the sun? If that was ever true, I don't remember it. Like I don't remember Dad this astonishingly handsome, or happy, or deeply in love with his wife.

HAVANA

Celia del Pino

Santa Teresa del Mar

After hurricane season, the island resumed its beautiful sameness of days, the December skies so flatly blue they looked catatonic. The sea was placid, too, as if inviting Celia to skate across its surface. A wisp of evening breeze stirred the hibiscus and coaxed perfume from her winter gardenia tree, lush with dowager blossoms. The beach looked unfamiliar today, though she'd stared at this view for a lifetime. Celia's arms trembled as she lifted her binoculars. She was too old to guard the coast anymore but continued out of habit.

The hours passed but Celia didn't grow tired. She was absorbed by the savage ardor coursing through her veins, by the dreams she had started dreaming again: of leaving Cuba, of visiting her ex-lover in Granada, of dancing, if only for one night, in a swirl of skirts and red carnations. Never mind her litany of ailments. At the preposterously old age of ninety, her body—what was left of it, anyway—longed to join his.

Gustavo's third letter arrived yesterday, with its noisy tambourines of words. This time he included a plane ticket to Spain and generous funds for incidentals. Incidentals? What was incidental about traveling five thousand miles to visit a ghost? Celia sighed. So what if they met again and thoroughly humiliated themselves? What damn difference would it make? Long ago she'd learned a useful lesson: heartbreak couldn't kill her. If it managed to do so now, it would barely hasten the inevitable.

The radio replayed El Líder's famous Missile Crisis speech, part of a late-night parade of his greatest hits. From the onset of la revolución, the Yankees had insulted and assaulted the island to no end, persisting with their dirty tricks to this day. Yet the once-trustworthy Soviet Union abandoned them, too, in the end. After its collapse—overnight, it seemed to Celia—Cuba's economy ground to a halt. The ensuing "Special Period" kept the island in a state of acute uncertainty for a decade. Everyone blamed El Líder, but how was it his fault? Perestroika, glasnost—he'd had no use for any of it.

Celia snapped off the radio. The air contracted without the oxygen of El Líder's voice. The first filament of light seeped along the horizon, illuminating her stretch of beach. She often felt lonely at this hour. Her grandchildren were dispersed around the globe, and two of her three grown children were long dead. Only the imperious Lourdes was alive and retired in Miami, among the gusanos. Celia pictured her bakery-empresario daughter parked before a mountain of pastelitos, intent on devouring every last one.

Celia pushed herself off the wicker swing and limped to the bedroom. Her hips had grown stiffer from her stay at the hospital. She slipped off her housedress and stood naked before the full-length mirror, cracked and mottled, its metal fasteners rusted in place. Before cataract surgery, Celia's view of herself had been hazy, more distant memory than fact. Now her once gray-streaked hair looked like a sparse flag of surrender and the mole formerly buttoned to her cheek clung to the edge of her jaw.

Y, coño, when had her neck collapsed?

She rotated in place, resisting the urge to close her eyes, and inspected the aged spectacle of herself. Pues, time had done to her what it did to everyone—and it hadn't been timid about its claims. Why should she be any different? Celia was missing her left breast but at least she still had her teeth! On the wall behind her was the portrait Pilar had painted of Celia during her visit in 1980. Naturally, Celia had requested a bit of retouching: darker, more luxuriant hair; a slender waist; a less severe expression. ¡Qué vanidad!

Déjame en un ansia de oscuros planetas,
pero no me enseñes tu cintura fresca.

In this last letter Gustavo vowed to send a current photograph of himself if Celia promised to do the same. Was he crazy? Neither of them would move an inch off their rockers if they did that! Out of gentlemanly tact, perhaps, Gustavo had made no mention of their rapturous days at the Hotel Inglaterra, focusing instead on their lofty conversations, their love of García Lorca's poetry, the sublime arroz con cangrejos they'd dined on every night. Not a word about Celia boldly signing the hotel registry as his wife. Or his toying with the intricacies of her pink satin garter belt. Or their vigorous, every-which-way lovemaking before the mirrored mahogany armoire.

Celia had committed their hotel room to memory. The sagging double beds, the checkered tiled floors, the spindly table on which they'd played late-night dominoes (she won every game). The shuttered floor-to-ceiling windows had opened onto a wrought-iron balcony overlooking the Parque Central, which was lively day and night with passersby. A trio of musicians from Santiago de Cuba played the popular "Lágrimas Negras" on the hour.

A passion like theirs was never meant to last. Never meant to be domesticated, or yoked to raising children, or paying taxes. Its very nature was fleeting. Over the years Celia had consoled herself with this lie: that it had been better for them to have parted when they did, when Gustavo could return to Spain—to his war, to his wife, to a future without her. Their interlude in Havana would remain forever an untainted ideal. Until now.

"I want to be beautiful for us again," Celia whispered to the mirror. Desire was scratching at her like a tiny ghost crab. And no, she would *not* leave Cuba after nearly a century only to have an amicable tea with Gustavo. ¡Qué va!

Celia walked naked into the living room and wrapped herself in the moth-eaten mantilla draped over the upright walnut piano. The piano was bleached a chalky white from an eternity of sunlight and sea air, and hadn't been tuned in decades—keys sharp in some places, flat or dead in others. Despite its flaws, Celia sat and played the opening to Debussy's "La Soirée dans Grenade" with great delicacy.

Herminia pushed open the front door, carrying two bamboo cages filled with jittery bullfinches. "So, I see you've decided to go to Spain, eh?"

"Maybe." Celia shyly covered her missing breast with a corner of the mantilla.

"Pero, niña, you look raring to go!" Herminia teased. She would no sooner discourage Celia than stand on her head. "Did you write him back yet?"

Celia looked away, hesitant to confess.

"¡Candela eres!" Herminia clapped her hands. "I wish I could go with you and find un viejito rico for myself!"

The bullfinches frantically flapped their wings, too anxious to sing. They were comely birds, indigenous to the island, arguably its best warblers—and diminishing in numbers. Herminia captured the birds in the mountains of Pinar del Río but Celia didn't ask why. It was better not to know too much. If the police came around asking questions, she could vouch for Herminia, say whatever it took to prevent her arrest. Celia made a mental note to write a character reference for her neighbor's official files. As a former people's judge in Santa Teresa del Mar, she knew her word still counted for something.

Herminia escorted her back to the bedroom and helped her into a fresh housedress, tube socks, and her last pair of battered sneakers. Then she combed out Celia's hair, twisting it into an outmoded chignon.

"Do we have any hair dye?" Celia smoothed a flyaway strand.

"I can find you some tomorrow."

"Jet black?"

"Unless you're planning to go platinum blond? ¿Como la Marilyn Monroe?"

Celia laughed. She was grateful to Herminia for emboldening her to risk love again. Twenty years ago she'd walked into the ocean expecting to die, surrendering the drop-pearl earrings Gustavo had given her. But after losing consciousness, she floated to shore like a sodden log of driftwood. Herminia found her, saved her, became the only one who didn't leave her.

The two women made their way to the back porch. A dragonfly lingered over the bird-of-paradise. The wind was picking up, rustling the fronds of the royal palms. A squadron of pelicans took turns catapulting into the surf while a pair of storm petrels squabbled over a stranded crab. The clouds looked like dirty rags in the distance.

"¿Cafecito?"

"Gracias, Herminia."

Already, the day felt ancient. Celia resettled on her wicker swing and aimed her binoculars at the horizon. Here, at the edge of the Caribbean, anything seemed possible, forgivable. Was she imagining Gustavo's face hovering in the distance, his lips immense and pliant, murmuring poetry to her in the breeze: *Verde que te quiero verde . . .*

Long ago, Celia had asked herself which was worse: separation or death? Death was the ultimate separation, sin duda. But to be forced apart, exiled, torn from those she loved? That was worse, far worse. Celia lowered her binoculars and studied the waves racing toward shore, racing toward her.

2

Herminia Delgado

Santa Teresa del Mar

I woke up very early on the day of our departure. A trusted neighbor drove me east. We said nothing on the way. No questions, no small talk. We both understood that silence was her best protection. As payment I gave Gladys my bamboo cages and disclosed my best trapping spots in Pinar del Río. The demand for Cuban bullfinches was soaring. Dealers were smuggling them into Miami—drugged and pinned inside plastic hair curlers—then selling them to nostalgic exiles who paid fortunes to hear the birds sing in their own kitchens.

I hated to leave Cuba without telling Celia. How would she get along without me? I cooked for her every day, took her to the doctor, kept her company most nights on her porch. We didn't say much. It was enough not to be alone. Last week I found Celia under the tamarindo, knocking fruit out of the tree with her great-aunt's parasol (also used as a cane). Bueno, I turned those tamarindos into jam with sugar and boiling water.

Celia became a die-hard revolutionary back in the fifties, when El Líder was fighting in the Sierra Maestra. How could she understand my wanting to abandon the island for good? Of course, she was toying with the idea of visiting her old lover in Spain but I doubted she'd be gone for long. What I hoped, for her sake, was that the Spaniard could still please Celia the way he once had. ¡Jaja! As a last favor, I dyed her hair blue-black as a crow's.

It was still dark when my neighbor dropped me off on a deserted road, then turned around for home. I picked my way along the rocky shore until I met up with my traveling companions. We were a group of twelve religiosos—eleven men and me. Los doce apóstoles, some-one joked. We'd worked hard to prepare our boat: reinforcing the sails with strips of leather; adapting a Russian Lada's engine; strength-ening the hull with planks stolen from park benches in Matanzas.

We raised a blue flag in honor of Yemayá, goddess of the seas. As we pushed off, we sang to her for protection: *Yemayá Asesu, / Asesu Yemayá, / Yemayá Olodo, / Olodo Yemayá* . . . The ocean was choppy but the forecast stayed favorable: overcast with no rain and steady, northerly winds. Our plan was to make decent headway by nightfall. It was then that people lost their nerve, let fear get the bet-ter of them. But our chances were good, better than good, because we had the orishas on our side.

Our first hours at sea felt blessed and free. But by midafternoon our engine stopped. No amount of praying or tinkering—and with ace mechanics on board!—could fix it. The waves cracked against the sides of our boat, a matchstick in the immensity. We took turns at the oars, led by our babalawo, whose neck muscles bulged from the effort. "¡Yemayá nos acompaña!" he rallied us. It was tough, hand-splintering work. As the day faded to dusk, a bank of clouds obscured the moon.

The night grew blacker than the blackest apagón, blacker than a closed coffin, blacker than the deepest parts of the sea. We rowed and prayed through that blackness, ignoring our bleeding palms, fighting a terror colder than the night. I thought about Felicia as I rowed. If our journey failed I'd soon be playing dominoes with her on a roving cloud somewhere. Better that than returning to Cuba!

The government's coffers were dry. Nobody got their share of rations anymore, except for sugar. Everything else—eggs, milk, plátanos, tinned meat—vanished off the shelves or landed in the black market at astronomical prices. There was no gas either. You needed dollars for that. The Party faithful were rewarded with Chinese Pigeon bicycles, which caused countless accidentes in Havana. The rest of us had to wait hours for a bus, or walk. And we lost weight—thirty pounds, on average!

By dawn the skies looked more promising. The winds had tattered Yemayá's flag but we were still in one piece. Then out of nowhere a fleet of seabirds appeared, drifting above us, as if calculating our odds of survival. They were peculiar birds, unlike any I'd seen before, bright blue, with beaks like shiny trumpets. Were they a hallucination of angels? Had they come to announce our triumph, or our defeat?

One bird plummeted into the sea and surfaced with a thrashing mackerel. It was the blood from this fish that brought on what came next. From its dorsal fin and the expanse of its back, we could tell it was un monstruo. What if it rammed our boat, flipped it over, made of us a tidy meal? As believers, we had to trust in the orishas more than we trusted ourselves. Otherwise what did faith mean? I was a daughter of Changó, the most powerful of the gods, but I'd be lying if I said I didn't suffer a crisis of faith now and then.

The shark followed us until noon, then veered west. But our troubles weren't over. Just ahead, falling apart in the sea, were the remnants of a boat. Fifty yards on, another lancha was floating in pieces. The dead motor, the shark, now the empty boats. We knew what this meant: our trip was cursed.

I worked up courage by thinking about my son, who'd navigated a sailboat to Florida last year in eleven hours flat. On Sunday, Eusebio and I were talking on the phone about ordinary things—the latest baseball scores, his work at the pillow factory, the mattress he was buying on installment, nuevo de paquete. He had no idea I was planning to leave Cuba. Why should I worry him? Or tempt the spies who monitored long-distance calls?

At precisely four o'clock, as if by appointment, a ship rose out of the seas like a mirage. It was the U.S. Coast Guard, with a row of men in white uniforms on its prow. Our hearts sank so hard and so fast that I was surprised our boat didn't collapse from the collective despair. Carajo, we were just thirty-six miles from Key West.

I had half a mind to throw myself overboard—to swim or drown, to resist capture. The babalawo passed around a bottle of rum to steady our nerves. A Spanish-speaking officer informed us that we'd be taken to the U.S. military base in Guantánamo to be "processed." Así, como sardinas en lata.

It was back to Cuba for me, back to Santa Teresa del Mar, back to my fate—however difficult, however unwanted.

BERLIN

I

Ivanito Villaverde

Leipzig, Germany

Ivanito was exhausted after three days of back-to-back events at the European Translators Association conference. He couldn't remember much from last night's blowout party, either, except for the vodka shots and the man with a prosthetic eye who'd ended up in his hotel bed. Ilya, was it? Another Russian, of course. He had a weakness for them. Even the most brutish read Chekhov and were appealingly fatalistic. Whatever he and the Russian had done last night had his every joint aching.

Ivanito strained to focus on his panel: "The Perils of Simultaneous Translation." The other panelists were stupefyingly loquacious, making it impossible to get a word in. The mishaps he'd witnessed over the years had been farcical, like the time that Russian oligarch's pet bear intruded on his banya conclave with British officials, or when those German arborists came to blows on the contentious subject of spruce bark beetles (who knew?).

"Would you mind repeating that?" Ivanito addressed the audience member who'd asked him a question.

"I said, what do you do when one client disparages another and expects you to translate word for word?"

"You're asking if *mistranslation* can be a deliberate strategy?"

"Precisely."

"We're translators. Conduits, nothing more." Ivanito's temples thrummed from the hangover and his pinging halo. "Utmost accuracy is crucial for communication. It's not our job to influence the outcome."

"But aren't we also cultural translators?" the Italian panelist interjected with a note of hostility. "Our responsibility is to facilitate communication, not just be word machines."

These panels were so predictable, Ivanito thought, recycling the same self-serving ideas with the earnestness of freshman philosophy students. But nobody became relevant by merely wishing themselves to be. If these translators were so desperate for the limelight, they should try stepping onto a bare stage in a spangled gown and stilettos. That would get them the attention they craved!

"We stand on the edge of everything important," Ivanito continued, "but we're expected to remain invisible. That's our job."

It was this chameleon invisibility that he loved best about translation work—losing himself in the camouflage of other languages, other identities, its possibilities for reinvention. Maybe translating was just a more respectable form of drag?

Foreign languages had always been easy for him, like geometry problems no one else could solve. Growing up in 1970s Cuba meant Russian lessons in elementary school, Russian cartoons in the afternoons (*Los Muñequitos Rusos*), and magazines devoted to Soviet news (*Novedades de Moscú, Tiempos Nuevos, Sputnik*). Best of all, he loved how Russian sounded. His first teacher, Mr. Mikoyan, encouraged his talent. "Perfect—it is perfect!" he would say, praising Ivanito's spelling, his accent, his recitation of a poem. Eventually, he felt more at home in Russian literature than any place he'd actually lived.

Ivanito frequently switched among his four languages, which occupied distinct internal geographies. Spanish was his most vulnerable tongue, reserved for the deep terrain of childhood and García Lorca's poetry (a love he shared with Abuela Celia). Cursing was most effective in English, by far, thanks to tutorials from Pilar when he was a teenager. Russian was his default language in matters of truth—immortal *istina*, not everyday *pravda* (as Nabokov had remarked). Plus he revered its intricate verb declensions.

Cruising and nostalgia felt most natural to him in German. Ivanito was particularly fond of German's tongue-twisting agglutinations: concepts built from disparate, strung-together parts. Lebensabschnittpartner ("the person I'm with today"), for example, or Backpfeifengesicht ("a face in need of a fist"), both of which came in handy when cruising in Berlin. And German had a trove of nouns for *nostalgia* (die Sehnsucht, das Heimweh, die Wehmut . . .), which described with nuance the complexities of his lifelong dislocations. How Ivanito fit in everywhere, and nowhere, at once.

The translators grew more agitated as they argued—arms flailing, hairpins flying, jackets thrown off as if spoiling for a fight. If they'd had gauntlets, they would've thrown them down, too, challenged one another to old-fashioned duels. (Ivanito thought of poor Pushkin, a serial duelist, mortally wounded by his wife's seducer.) Translators were typically a steady bunch, unflappable under pressure. But not today. He hadn't seen them so stirred up since last year's panel "Prepositional Perplexities."

Ivanito's halo pinged louder as the debates raged. Was he imagining it playing the opening notes to Bach's first cantata? They were in Leipzig, after all. Or was his mother orchestrating yet another disturbance to derail his focus? Was she really convinced that she owned his life, even now? And how could Mami, who'd been incapable of the most mundane tasks when she was alive, pull this off? Did everyone get superpowers when they died? Could you choose which ones you wanted?

Ivanito poured himself a glass of water from the pitcher on

the table. It refreshed him, eased the burning sensation in his scalp. An ice pack would've been preferable. He recalled something Mr. Mikoyan had told him once, paraphrasing Pushkin: *If I want to understand you, I must study your obscure language.* But how was it possible to translate a solitary word from one language to another without its rich, cultural matrix—phonetic, semantic, historical?

And in no tongue, Ivanito thought miserably, were there adequate words for how his world was collapsing.

On the train back to Berlin, Ivanito began rereading Goncharov's *Oblomov,* which no shortage of critics had dismissed as tedious in the extreme. The novel's hapless hero was so inert that he moved just once in the first fifty pages—from his bed to a chair. Inaction supplanted conflict, yet the story was engaging, hilarious, self-skewering, unsparing of the human condition—in short, quintessentially Russian. It made Ivanito long to crawl into bed and spend the rest of his life fretting under the covers.

The conifer forests flew by in shadowed, aggregate greens interspersed with vast blankets of snow. Here was the famed winter countryside of Germany, a far cry from the royal palms of his tropical boyhood. As he leaned back against the headrest, Ivanito recalled a trip he and Mami had taken to a labyrinth of underground caves in Matanzas, which were teeming with blind fish. Those creatures had adapted remarkably to their lightless environment, something he and his mother could never do.

Like her, Ivanito didn't believe in utopias or isms of any kind. When did power ever *not* turn to violence and oppression? Every political system imprisoned language, outlawed independent thinking, reduced meaning to slogans. From the rigid dogmas of the Cuban Revolution—with its homophobic pronouncements and camps for "degenerados"—to his tía Lourdes's capitalist tirades and anti-Russian everything. His aunt went so far as denouncing Dezik and Tsygan, the first Soviet space dogs!

In his view, Gogol had infinitely more to say than Marx.

Ivanito purchased two small cartons of milk from the ambulant vendor on the train. Milk had been a rarity in Cuba, prioritized for nursing mothers and toddlers. As a boy, he'd been tasked with milking the cows in his boarding school's barn outside San Antonio de los Baños. He'd welcomed the peace of that barn: the owl in the rafters scanning for rats; the ribbon of fruit bats uncoiling at dusk; the cows' yielding udders filling his tin pail to the brim. Frequently, he'd aimed a stream of warm milk into his mouth.

But it was in that same barn that the bully José María Fugaz and his lackeys choked him to near-unconsciousness. Then they pushed him facedown in the filthy hay and pulled down his red Pioneer shorts. The bewildered cows lowed in their stalls as the boys fell against him, one rougher than the next, splitting him in two. They forced their pingas inside him—hard and thick as stalks of sugarcane. Ivanito nearly passed out from the pain. He tried to imagine snow falling in cold waves around him, willed himself to float upward, high above his body, a rogue snowflake against the blizzarding rest.

Finally, Fugaz zipped his pants and spat on Ivanito, disgusted by his submission. He and the other boys jammed handfuls of hay into his mouth, warning Ivanito to say nothing if he didn't want more of the same. *Huevón. Maricón. Pato de porquería.* They left, laughing and joking. It was February and Ivanito could smell the tobacco from the surrounding fields, ready for harvest. The hay's sharp edges cut his mouth and hidden slivers of glass slashed his knee. His eyes burned from holding back tears.

Afterward he came close to hanging himself—carefully arranging the stool, the belt, the solitude. (A senior had hanged himself in the toolshed a month before, showing the way.) Only the image of Mami's face kept him from kicking over the stool. He was six years old.

⸻◦⸻

It was late afternoon when the train pulled into the Zoologischer Garten station. When Ivanito had moved to Berlin in 1992—after a grueling two-day train ride from Moscow—it was a wild place, an encampment of fugitives. After the Wall fell, thousands of young people from around the world flooded into the city to reimagine their lives. Ivanito immediately joined a commune, a collection of outsiders like him, who'd taken over an abandoned building in Mitte. Many survived by selling chiseled-off pieces of the Wall to tourists in Potsdamer Platz.

Every day he and his fellow squatters—punks, artists, cross-dressers, drug addicts, even a Che Guevara look-alike—foraged for food, scavenged junkyards for treasures, jerry-rigged everything from toilets to generators. Ivanito's biggest score: an aluminum Soviet-era tub from the seventies. It became the commune's signature possession. Another prized find was the neon green APOTHEKE sign that he managed to revive with illegally siphoned electricity.

At night Berlin was rife with fanatical partying: action theater, raves, drag shows, performance art, dance clubs (Wunderbar, Tresor), drugs (Ecstasy, speed, ketamine, LSD), and a boggling array of take-your-pick kink fests (BDSM, fetishes galore, erotic asphyxiation at Cabaret O_2). The single operating principle? Vor allem Freude! Only money was scarce. Ivanito bought clothes by the pound at secondhand shops and ate enough communal lentil soup to keep him chronically flatulent.

The city had been built on swamplands and the ruins of war, but to him it looked a lot less apocalyptic than parts of Havana, which were crumbling from the Revolution's neglect. There hadn't been a major conflict on Cuba's shores since the Wars of Independence, unless you counted the Bay of Pigs invasion. But that fiasco had taken place far from the capital and lasted all of forty-eight hours. In fact, his own mother was conscripted to fight in the Zapata Swamp and issued a rifle she didn't have a clue how to use.

Ivanito soon grew tired of Berlin's economies of scarcity—reminiscent of the island's byzantine barter system—and took a translation job with a German bank for a stretch. The salary enabled him to move to Charlottenburg, on the settled western side of the city, and solidify his finances after years of penury. The apartment he chose was as bourgeois as they came—down to the striped velour wallpaper and walk-in closet. It was a relief to live in one place after mariposiando from country to country.

Over the next seven years, Ivanito painstakingly collected Bauhaus furniture, Meissen porcelain, and fire-sale imports from Special Period Cuba. He preferred the authentic life of objects over the falsities of history. Objects were testaments to their age—and never lied. His most cherished acquisition? A 1920s mirrored mahogany armoire, said to have come from an elegant hotel in Havana, and which seemed to hold time itself in its contours. How something so large and ungainly ended up in Berlin was a mystery.

But what made Ivanito feel truly at home was his jungle of tropical plants: rubber trees and philodendron, a Cuban raintree (*Brunfelsia nitida*), peace lilies, aloe vera, begonias, myriad ferns, ribbon dracaena, and a pair of Nun's hood orchids. Each plant required specific care—aeration, misting, topsoil-resurfacing—plus hours of nurturing classical music. Mozart's *Così Fan Tutte* seemed to perk up the lot of them best.

The little jungle kept his island roots close, but not too close. And the plants needed a fair amount of heating in winter, for which Ivanito paid his grumbling, war-widow landlady—with her broad Berlin accent and mothballed stench—a monthly supplement. It was worth every Pfennig. Nowadays he earned a living as a freelance translator and adjunct professor. It could be precarious

at times, but immensely more satisfying than working at that stul-
tifying bank.

Performing drag was the icing.

On his way home, Ivanito swung by KaDeWe to pick up a lipstick
from his friend's cosmetics counter. In her youth, Dagmar Trapp had
looked remarkably like Eva Braun, Hitler's last mistress—and she'd
cultivated the likeness with chin-length curls and a pair of Scottish
terriers. Dagmar had married three men successively, each profess-
ing elation at posthumously cuckolding der Führer. The husbands
had left her materially comfortable for the rest of her life.

"Now, hold still," Dagmar said, applying liquid eyeliner. "This
is the trickiest part." Behind her thick vintage cat-eye glasses, her
eyes looked like guppies in a bowl. Yet her hands were steady for a
woman her age (seventies, he guessed). Then Dagmar double-coated
his lashes with high-volume mascara and surveyed her handiwork.

"Perfekt!" She brushed Ivanito's hair back from his temples. "Ach,
but your head is so hot! Too much thinking, my friend."

Ivanito hadn't expected a makeover, but he was pleased with the
results—a boost after the dispiriting translation conference. He
toyed with the idea of telling Dagmar about his halo but decided
against it. Why complicate their relationship?

"So, when's your next show?" She slipped a sample of French
perfume into his pocket.

"In June. You'll be the first on my guest list."

"Sicher, Liebe." They pecked good-bye without smudging each
other's makeup.

Ivanito dropped off his roller bag at home, then headed straight
to his regular hookup spot in the Tiergarten. An alluringly sullen
man cruised him outside the men's toilet. He was just Ivanito's type,
too: well over six feet, semi-emaciated yet muscular, hair cropped
close to his skull, pale eyes as liquid as his Russian dancer's. There

was a daisy in the buttonhole of his vest, a nice touch amid the rivet-studded leather.

Everything was settled with a look. No names, no words, zero kissing. Alles war verboten. Ivanito preferred to be on the receiving end of rough. The stranger shoved him face-first against the back wall of the cinder-block building. Broken glass glittered at their feet. Was he imagining the taste of hay? They fumbled with belts and zippers, the requisite protection. Then came the salve of spit, a fierce separation of flesh, the hard thrusting that completed them both.

Irina del Pino

Berlin

It was a frenzied opening day at Irina's gleaming sportswear factory in the Scheunenviertel neighborhood of Berlin: VIP factory tours; a morning press conference; the ribbon-cutting ceremony with that lecherous Russian ambassador. Already, the European Union's finest department stores—KaDeWe, Les Galeries Lafayette, Harrods, La Rinascente—had sent an avalanche of orders. And this week's *Stern* magazine featured a two-page spread of a sultry, supine Irina under the headline RUSSIA'S HOTTEST ENTREPRENEUR!

After the festivities, Irina threw on her ermine coat and went for a stroll along the Spree River. Ferries and tugboats churned through the waters with a stately air. It was early March—wet, raw, and gray—but still a lot warmer than Moscow. Irina bought a lamb shish kebab from a riverside vendor. As she sat on a bench, a red admiral butterfly landed on her thigh. It reminded her of mushroom hunting with her mother in the swampy woodlands outside Moscow. Of course, that was her *childhood* mother. By the time Irina was expelled from high school for kissing girls, Maminka had volunteered for the war in Afghanistan, leaving behind her dead-end nursing job and a disastrous marriage.

Her parting words: *It can't be worse than the hell at home.*

Hooded crows gathered atop a linden tree, looking like tuxedoed

musicians on a break. Irina swung one arm up like an orchestra con-
ductor but the crows didn't budge. She hardly knew Berlin except
for the environs of the Hotel Adlon, where she'd been staying for the
past three weeks. The sight of yellow cranes meant she was facing
east, toward the endless construction of unification.

How many borders had fallen in her lifetime? The Berlin Wall,
the far-flung boundaries of the USSR, the shifting puzzle of the
former Soviet bloc. Nothing lasted forever. Nichego.

Irina finished her skewer of lamb. The sound of a distant accor-
dion drew her a kilometer downriver, where she discovered a hundred or so women dancing tango in an open-air tent. They swiveled
this way and that, their torsos regally still, their footwork intricate
on the portable parquet. As their shapely legs flashed, it looked
as if the dancers were toying with fleeing their upper halves. Irina
was entranced by the carnal glow of their bodies, by the shape-
shifting dusk and the red carnations scattered on the plastic cocktail
tables.

She lit a gold-tipped cigarette, languidly blowing smoke out
the side of her mouth. A quartet of female musicians—violinist,
keyboardist, bandoneonista, vocalist—were performing a plangent
lament:

> Igual que aquella noche tan lejana
> Es esta de mi amarga soledad . . .

A stocky, soft butch, leading a gap-toothed femme in a clingy
dress, puckered her lips at Irina. Another in a camel suede suit propo-
sitioned her outright: Komm mit mir weg, Liebling. She was intrigued
by the woman's swagger—not unlike the fencers she'd known—but
it was too soon to commit to the night's erotic adventures.

"Wo sind wir?" she asked the trans bartender. Irina's German was
serviceable after a year with a private tutor back home.

"Tangolandia," the bartender said, introducing herself as Trudi.

"Didn't you know? They're all champions here." She pointed to a dancer with a bandaged ear, whispering that her partner—the one with a mermaid tattoo on her face—had bit it off in a jealous rage.

Irina ordered a beer and tucked a ten-mark tip into Trudi's apron. Then she sat back to watch the dancing. Most couples adhered to strict gender roles; a few embraced looser self-expressions. And though the dance floor was packed, each pair kept a perfect, revolving distance from everyone else. The effect was hypnotic, kaleidoscopic. If she could open a queer club like this in Moscow, she'd make another fortune.

The beer was lukewarm. Normally, Irina would've complained, but today wasn't a day for complaining. Her sportswear venture was a success and soon Caress would become a household name in Europe. The Russian economy might be in turmoil but she expected the Old Guard and the Novi Ruski to resolve their political battles for business's sake. Maybe their new president, Vladimir Putin, could put things right? Anyone was better than that oafish Yeltsin.

There was no room for the irrational in Irina's life, so what she saw next stole her breath. Lingering at the far end of the dance floor was an exact replica of herself staring back. The stranger was dressed in a sailor suit, her cap concealing most of her short, wavy hair. But their overall assemblage of flesh and bones was identical. Was she a figment of Irina's imagination? The manifestation of fatigue? What was the German word for this anomaly?

"Doppelgänger," the sailor said, now standing before her. She extended her hand as if reaching for Irina from the depths of a mirror. "Dance with me, Liebe."

"I can't—" The woman's touch sent a flame up Irina's arm and settled in her clavicle like a live coal. Without a word, she followed her twin to the dance floor.

"Don't be afraid," the doppelgänger murmured as their duplicate foreheads merged. "Lean into me. I won't let you fall."

Was it possible to dance with yourself? Irina bruised a hip from the effort, tripping over her feet. Her superb balance from fencing was of little help. The twins brought their faces as close together as possible without kissing, though it was tempting to kiss. The confusion and attraction were irresistible. As a schoolgirl Irina used to practice kissing in a handheld mirror, fantasizing that it was a pretty classmate kissing her back.

"Bist du meine Schwester?" Irina's accent was pronounced.

The doppelgänger smiled and answered in Russian. "Who else could I be?"

They settled at an empty table and ordered a bottle of Patagonian malbec. Moonlight illuminated their high foreheads, their reflective gestures. The tango dancers swirled past them in a seductive haze, but the twins were too hypnotized by each other to notice. When Irina looked left, Tereza looked right, cradling their chins in opposite palms like sepaled blooms. They were mirror-image twins. Neveroyatnyy!

"When's your birthday?" Irina asked.

Her sister hesitated before answering. "I suspect it's the same as yours."

"May ninth, 1971?"

They were too stunned to speak.

"Where?" Irina finally asked.

"Prague."

"Fucking hell!" She felt as if her mother's Soviet-era iron were pressing down on her chest. "Why didn't we know about each other until now?"

"Or how we were separated?" Tereza, too, was indignant. "And why?"

"Who's to blame for this?"

They spoke in a rush of German and Russian, trying to piece together their histories: of who was where, when, and with whom. Was there the remotest possibility that they might have met before tonight? Or was this accidental meeting all they had?

Tereza, an archivist, grew up in East Berlin believing that her father was Argentine, a union organizer who'd met her German mother in Prague. Irina insisted that *her* father was Cuban and had met her Czech mother in Prague that same summer. Back in Moscow, she had a photograph of Javier del Pino holding her as an infant. Wasn't that proof enough?

Close to midnight the twins returned to the dance floor for a last milonga. Their initial awkwardness gave way to an easy fusion of rib cages, of intertwining limbs, until Irina could no longer tell where her body ended and her sister's began.

3

Ivanito Villaverde

Berlin

By midmorning Ivanito was on the dregs of his second pot of coffee. A faint light filtered in through the curtains. How drearily these March days affected his spirits! He was anxious, unfocused, seized by a creeping paralysis, and woefully behind on his work. Dozens of pages were strewn across his kitchen table: Tsvetaeva poems he was translating from Russian to Spanish for a publisher in Madrid; lesson plans for his Translation Fundamentals course at Freie Universität; sheafs of engineering terminology for an upcoming conference in Potsdam.

Since his mother's last visitation, Ivanito hadn't eaten or slept well, holing up in his apartment for weeks at a time, too wrecked to do anything. Gaunt, sleepless, morose—he was a bundle of nerves. He'd been out of sorts for so long that no routine seemed fitting. If he was hungry, he ate. If he was restless, he walked. If he was mournful, he played music. Even his little jungle of houseplants was drooping, as if reflecting his despair.

Whenever Ivanito dared glance in a mirror, his halo looked more deeply sunken into his skull. And there was no relief from its crushing pressure, or the intermittent migraines. The last one had forced him to cancel his appearance at the Mean Queen Drag Competition, which he'd handily won last year, performing Marlene Dietrich's "Ich Bin Die Fesche Lola" from *Der Blaue Engel*.

Where was his mother, anyway? Why had she upended his life, only to disappear again? Weren't ghosts supposed to have a mission—like Hamlet's father? Or was Mami lonely and simply wanting company? Were there no dominoes games to amuse her in the afterlife? Was she finding eternity boring? Had she depleted the other ghosts? Ivanito imagined his mother wandering high among the timeless clouds, or whistling toward him like an arrow aimed between his eyes. He knew nothing for certain except that he'd been bound to her in life and now, apparently, in death.

Ivanito poured himself a glass of warm milk to settle his stomach. Since the conference in Leipzig, he'd lost two more contracts—with the German Biophysical Society and the Hoteliers of Bavaria—due to professional negligence. And his translation students were complaining to the dean about his erratic absences. He would lose that position, too, if he wasn't careful. To make ends meet, he'd humbly agreed to write a multilingual tourist guide for St. Hedwig's Cathedral. Scheisse.

To console himself, Ivanito meticulously applied a full face of makeup, slipped into his custom-made gold lamé jumpsuit, and strapped on a pair of Lucite platforms. He felt most lavishly visible disguised as someone else. A successful drag show was fragile, a high-wire fantasy. One false move—wrong-era shoes, a mole out of place, a zipper where a row of buttons should be—and the illusion vanished. He took his time replicating his divas' iconic outfits with the help of the finest seamstress in Mitte. None of this was cheap. But the results were breathtaking. Why settle for anything less?

For his next premiere, Ivanito planned to impersonate La Lupe, the volcanic Cuban singer from the sixties and seventies. Fans had worshipped the diva for her histrionic, no-holds-barred style. Onstage she'd wept, moaned, screamed obscenities, pulled her hair, bitten herself, scratched her face, torn her clothes, grabbed her breasts, thrown her shoes at the audience—or deployed them to pummel her pianist. When her first husband likened her dancing to an epileptic fit, she promptly divorced him.

In the late fifties and early sixties, La Lupe headlined nightclubs from one end of Cuba to the other. Everyone called her crazy. Loca de remate. Her sexual boldness even threatened El Líder. When he shut down her Havana club and confiscated her Cadillac, La Lupe emigrated and became a bigger star in New York. But by the eighties, the diva was impoverished and living in the Bronx—crippled by a slew of show-business betrayals and a fall off a ladder while hanging curtains (the identical fate of Tolstoy's Ivan Ilyich!).

La Ivanita liberally sprayed herself with Gardénia, the diva's favorite perfume. To fully inhabit La Lupe meant knowing everything about her, from her nickname (La Yiyiyi) to her romantic type (violent, flattering hustlers) to her signature move (slapping her culo at the end of each show). La Ivanita danced in her platforms to "Este Mambo," then abruptly changed the mood with "La Tirana," a theatrical bolero, lip-synching to the lyrics:

> Según tu punto de vista
> Yo soy la mala—

"¿Qué haces?" A low-pitched voice emanated from the hallway.

Ivanito flinched before spying his mother in the Jugendstil mirror. "¡Por dios, Mami! You scared the hell out of me!"

"Lo siento, corazón," she said, coughing delicately into her wrist. Her face was oyster gray. Was this within normal range for a ghost?

"Are you okay?" Ivanito inched closer. "Where have you been?"

"In Belarus."

"What were you doing there?"

"What is anyone ever doing anywhere?" Mami shimmied out of

the mirror and stroked his cheek with an icy hand. Her hair was a bird's nest mess. "Déjame decirte, I didn't understand a word of their language. I'm not a polygraph like you."

"You mean a polyglot."

"Lo que sea. All this traveling has exhausted me."

Ivanito got a better look at his mother. She was almost life-size this time and wore a tattered housedress with pockets and a calico pañuelo. Her feet were squeezed into scuffed, colorless pumps. Her jaw looked slack, too, as if it had slipped off its hinges, and her teeth were yellower than he remembered. Nothing about her suggested ghost, or glamour, or mystery—just pura guajira.

"Your Spanish sounds funny," Mami said.

"Funny how?"

"All stuck up, like you're not from Cuba anymore."

"Bueno, I'm not."

"But it's your mother tongue!"

Ivanito didn't respond. Mami's mother tongue was limited and melodramatic. His Spanish was capable of prodigiously more.

"Ay, it's like the Sierra Maestra in here!" She surveyed the dense foliage. "When did you do this?"

"I've had these plants forever."

"I hadn't noticed." His mother settled on the sofa, tugged off her shoes, and massaged her dirty, swollen feet. "Have you heard from your sisters?"

"I only speak to Milagro de vez en cuando."

"You should try to get closer to them."

"Why?"

"Because we're family."

Ivanito grew defensive. "When was the last time you spoke with them?"

"It's not so easy," Mami said, picking her toes. "They've put up a brick wall I can't penetrate. They never needed me."

"That's been going on since childhood." His twin sisters were a sensitive topic. Luz and Milagro had nothing in common with anyone but themselves. It was as if they'd been dropped into their family by accident. Ivanito and his sisters looked so much alike—gangly limbs, short torsos, as if missing their floating ribs—that they could only be siblings.

"Talking about them depresses me, mijo. They don't understand me like you do."

Naturally, Mami wouldn't consider how she could've made the effort to understand them. Instead she changed the subject.

"You know, I could use some nicer clothes." Mami sounded reproachful, as if he were to blame for her sorry state.

Ivanito understood her distress—he hated not looking his best—and led her to his walk-in closet. Naturally, she gravitated to the most outlandish outfits, sampling them with a swish of her finger: his luxurious, mink-trimmed cape; one of the plumed headdresses Celia Cruz had worn performing at Carnegie Hall; a powder-blue, floor-length chiffon.

Finally, his mother decided on an emerald moiré gown with bell sleeves and topped it off with a platinum beehive wig. Delighted by what she called her "total look," Mami leaped into the air with self-admiration, then turned to ransack Ivanito's jewelry box. She helped herself to fake ruby clip-ons, a beaded diadem, and a fistful of gaudy rings.

Ivanito's verdict: she looked like a goddamn Christmas tree.

"I can help you freshen up your style, if that's what you want," he said diplomatically.

His mother ignored him. Not a peep about his own striking appearance either. She dug more deeply into Ivanito's closet and, to his chagrin, found his collection of supple leather whips, silk nooses, and the velvet-lined case with instruments designed for painful pleasure. She picked up a cat-o'-nine-tails by its thick, grooved handle and swung it with vigor.

Wistfully, it seemed to him.

Ivanito recalled his sisters' stories about their parents' violent outbursts—the black eyes, the split lips—but they'd separated months before he was born.

"Do you have chamomile tea?" Mami asked, her fingers twitching.

Wait. Did she just slip that sapphire ring into her mouth?

Ivanito set the water to boil. His mother stretched out on the sofa and dozed off—whether from her travels or her sartorial exertions, he wasn't sure. Hadn't Mami told him that she didn't need sleep? It surprised Ivanito that ghosts got tired at all. Wasn't it reasonable to assume that they'd have boundless energy? Weren't there any advantages to being dead? Ivanito held the tea under her nose until she sputtered awake.

"It's not real."

"What are you talking about?"

"The sapphire ring. It's a fake."

"Ah, bueno." His mother slipped it out of her cheek without apology, or saliva. Then she took a sip from the antique porcelain cup and stared at him. "¡Qué deslumbrante!"

Carajo. How had he forgotten his halo? "Get rid of it right now! It's destroying my life!"

"It's there to put things in perspective."

"It's crushing my skull! I can't accomplish a thing!"

"Nothing you're doing is important." Mami beamed as if she'd just complimented him.

"What are you talking about?"

"You don't belong here."

"But it's my life!"

Where would she have him live, then? Berlin was the only place Ivanito could tolerate after all his worlds had crashed—Cuba, New York, the Soviet Union.

"*Our* lives, mi cielo. We've always been one. You're only safe with me."

His mother was no different, dead or alive: incorrigible, capricious, egotistic.

"Can't you at least tell me where you are?"

"Geography means nothing where I am."

"Is there a hell?"

"Only on earth." His mother leaned toward him, her wig askew. "Which is much too dangerous for my boy. Now dance with me."

Ivanito took a step back. "I don't want to."

"But everything makes sense when we dance!"

Mami began singing and dancing by herself, enticing him to join her. *Quieres regresar, pero es imposible. / Ya mi corazón se encuentra rebelde* . . . It was their song, Beny Moré's "Corazón Rebelde." Ivanito knew it by heart, down to the distortions of the warped record she'd incessantly played that summer of coconuts.

"I'm not going back."

"Then go forward. With me."

"Espérate, Mami, you *chose* to die."

"I wouldn't say it was my choice." She continued swaying to the old bolero.

"Then whose choice was it?"

Again she stretched out her hands in invitation, but Ivanito refused her.

"I would say it was many things, mijo. It's true that I lost my will to live. But I didn't do anything to finish my life, either. Not like that first time."

Ivanito held back his tears. "I was just a boy."

"That's why I couldn't leave you behind. Who would've taken care of you?"

Ivanito remembered that sweltering day when his mother had served them bowls of coconut ice cream sprinkled with shards of lethal pink pills. It was lucky he'd been too drowsy to eat much. They held each other's gaze for a moment without rancor or fear.

It was tempting to surrender to her now, as he had as a boy. She'd explained to him once that the life force of every person was recycled into the universe when they died. That the dead became egun, ancestors who guided the living. If this was true, then how was she achieving this by wanting him dead, too?

"Ni modo, precioso." Her voice was a sweet elixir. "Come home."

"I am home."

His mother's mood shifted abruptly. She stopped dancing, emitted a savage little bark. A curious thrill raced through Ivanito's nervous system. He feared what she was capable of, her enduring power over him.

"You're here to kill me, then?"

"Ay, such violent language!" Warily, she took a closer look at him. "Think of everything that's happened to us, corazón. Really, did either of us need to suffer apart—and so extremely? We were much happier together."

"No, Mami. I'm happier now. On my own." Ivanito spread his arms wide, as if to say: *Look around you! Isn't this enough?*

"It doesn't seem so."

"You're not the arbiter of my life anymore!" He could argue with her in four languages but his mother would understand only what she wanted to hear. Even dead, she expected him to be solely what she needed.

"Death is alluring to you still."

"Is that what you came to tell me?"

"I'm offering you peace. Eternal peace."

"I can't believe this!" Ivanito wanted to shake her ghostly shoulders, rip off the fake ruby clip-ons, strip her of all the borrowed finery. "So, you're telling me you want to finish the job you botched when I was five?"

His mother stared at him, her face distorted by suffering. Ivanito knew that expression. It was the one that had made his ribs ache with guilt as a boy for not being a better son, for not saving her from herself. Is that why she'd plagued him with this damn halo? It was more than he could stand!

"I'm sorry, Mami." Ivanito unbuckled his platform shoes and settled next to her on the sofa. "Please stay. There's so much I need to know."

He longed to ask her questions, probe the pernicious rumors. Was it true that he'd been sent to boarding school *because* she'd tried to poison him? Had she really murdered a circus mechanic in Matanzas? And why had she disfigured his father's face with a skillet of sizzling oil? Ivanito had seen Papá just once—in bed with a masked whore in a shabby hotel room down by the Havana wharf.

But that was another story.

"That's not how it works." Mami's voice was fading, a scrap of wind.

"I can't ask my own dead mother questions?"

"It's time for us to reunite."

"Can't we meet up in, like, fifty years? After I've had a life of my own?"

Sparks began flying around his mother's waist, then rose to encircle her neck like a fiery choker. Was she short-circuiting?

"Te espero, mijo," she sighed, receding until she was no more than a pinprick of flame, a puff of air, the profound emptiness in her wake.

Ivanito sat immobilized for hours, watching the municipal buses trundle toward Bismarckstrasse. A sinister shadow crept over his begonias. Twilight appeared layered in veils, scarcely concealing the past, connecting him to flashbacks—Kriegsrückblicke—from World War II. The Jewish woman hidden in a Berlin sarcophagus by her husband. A Luftwaffe pilot fortifying himself with Pervitin before his next bombing mission. Prisoners hung by their wrists in the "singing forest" of Buchenwald.

As night fell, the rooftops of Charlottenburg blackened and the windows glowed from the blue television lights. Ivanito's chrome-and-glass grandfather clock pitilessly ticked. There was no misunderstanding his mother's intentions now. If she was determined to ensnare him with her "eternal peace" ruse, then what remained of his future? Could he battle the undertow of their past? Fight her and win?

Ivanito wiped his face clean of makeup and unzipped the gold lamé jumpsuit. Then he removed his wig, peeled off the fake eyelashes, and unbecame La Lupe. Stark naked, he stood before the mirrored mahogany armoire from faraway Havana. How slight and pale he looked without his diva accoutrements, like a snail parted from its shell. He splashed a bit of violet water on his wrists, inhaling its comforting scent.

After the rapes, Ivanito had grown obsessed with toxic flora, imagining himself a Venus flytrap vanquishing his enemies through his anus. He'd convinced himself that if he studied hard enough—became the best translator, the best *everything*—that his success would banish his shame. But it lurked in the spidery shadows of his consciousness, waiting to flare up and overwhelm him. It was like harboring an internal minefield.

Ivanito suspected that it was the surfeit of intimacies with his Russian lover that had augured the bitterness of their end. He regretted telling Sergei about the rapes (the only person he'd ever dared tell), about the wretched tangle of wanting and humiliation those bullies had provoked. But instead of showing compassion, Sergei had been disgusted, demanding why Ivanito hadn't fought back *like a man*. Chto? Fought off those bullies, who could've easily killed him and buried his boy's corpse in a tobacco field?

It wasn't Sergei's indiscretion with the ballerina that broke them up but his contempt for Ivanito. What had his ex-lover ever tasted of defeat? Onstage he'd danced as a prince, wielded magical powers, slain enemies with painted wooden swords. All without a hair out of place. Anguished over the end of their affair, and the dismantling of the country he'd loved—the literary idea of it, anyway—Ivanito departed Russia for good.

On the endless train ride from Moscow to Berlin, he reread railway tales from nineteenth-century Russian literature. The tragic fate of Chekhov's schoolteacher, Platonov. Turgenev's rhapsodic depictions of travels in the West. The last moment of Tolstoy's immortal Anna Karenina: " . . . *and the candle by which she had read the book of troubles, deceit, grief, and evil, flared up more brightly than ever before, illumed for her all that had been darkness, sputtered, began to dim and went out forever.*"

Mercifully, the stories eased Ivanito's spurned and halting heart. All the while, the train rumbled impassively toward its destination. His frigid window framed jackdaws and rooks in vast flocks, ponds frozen deep with somnolent fish, leafless birch trees, an anemic moon—visible at all hours—spectral excerpts of his face (like a displaced Narcissus). There were slow and ancient sleighs still in use, stubbled fields with ragtag scarecrows. Barking, monotonic dogs. A slaughterhouse. Ditches. Slovenly hovels. The whistling Arctic winds.

Ivanito alternately dozed, as if in a milky haze, or grew deliriously alert with memories he'd sooner forget. He and his fellow passengers studiously ignored one another, as if by silent accord. His stomach felt queasy; he could barely ingest more than a bit of dry bread dipped in watery soup, or tea from the onboard samovar. The diesel train stank of coal from the obsolete boilers heating the compartments. And every mile of his journey, every desolate station—the leaden skies spitting snow—was blurred by his grief.

⌐‿⌐

Back at the kitchen table, Ivanito surveyed the work he had no energy to complete. What if he were to disappear altogether? Who would miss him? Would his fans hold vigils for him outside Chez Schatzi?

Light candles in his name? He smiled to think of his funeral service, overflowing with Berlin's most flamboyant drag queens. Would catfights break out over his costume collection? Shouldn't he write up a last will and testament?

Ivanito pulled a carton of coconut ice cream from the freezer, recalling that grievous night on Palmas Street. His mother had whitened her face like a geisha's, painted on arched eyebrows, coated her lips a bright orange. Then she'd dusted Ivanito with talcum powder and dressed him in short pants and his Sunday jacket. *You must imagine winter, mijito, winter and its white extinguishings.* Ivanito closed his eyes and pictured snowflakes falling on everything he knew, a wintry utopia, like that photo essay in *Sputnik,* "The Snows of Mother Russia."

It seemed to Ivanito that he'd spent his whole life searching for that same ravishing numbness. He reclined on the sofa, filling in his mother's departed outline. Then he nestled under his eiderdown comforter and whispered lines of Tsvetaeva's:

> *Today or tomorrow the snow will melt.*
> *You lie alone beneath an enormous fur.*

MIAMI

1

Lourdes Puente

Miami

Sometimes when you asked, life gave you answers. Gone were Lourdes's empty, melancholic days on Key Biscayne, playing dominoes at the yacht club, listlessly shopping or getting her hair and nails done. No longer did she suffer the derision of Miami Cubans, who use to tease her about her "petrified" Spanish after decades in New York, or questioned her cubanidad. Nor did they look down at her anymore for owning a Brooklyn bakery that sold sticky buns instead of coconut flan.

Lourdes had become a respected leader in the exile community. A warrior—sí, a modern-day Joan of Arc—fighting to save the life of one small, vulnerable boy. As Eliseo González's new Miami spokesperson, she was at the epicenter of a titanic political battle. Nowadays she spent hours strategizing with Republican Congresswoman Ileana Sin-Luz, huddling with the top brass of the Cuban American National Foundation, and consulting daily with the González family's lawyers. When she asked Eliseo to swing a baseball bat, or sing the national anthem for the TV cameras, he readily complied. He was her boy now, the one she'd always dreamed of having.

Last month, Lourdes treated Eliseo and his uncles to an overnight visit to Disney World. El niño raced from ride to ride, ate junk food to his heart's content (no vegan anything at the Magic Kingdom), and could simply be a carefree boy. Meanwhile his uncles drank themselves into a stupor and flirted indecently with the female cartoon characters. *¡Dáme un besito, Minnie! ¡No me atormentes más!*

Eliseo's only setback was panicking at the "It's a Small World" boat ride. His shrieks echoed throughout the theme park, prompting Disney security, with their Mickey Mouse badges, to rush over. Lourdes had to prove to them that she wasn't kidnapping, or otherwise harming, the boy.

"Is it going to sink?" Eliseo cried between hiccups. "Is it, Tata?"

"No, mi cielo." Lourdes tried to put him at ease. "And you don't have to get on, if you don't want." Relieved, he clung to her for the rest of the day.

It'd been four months since Eliseo had lost his mother at sea, but he rarely spoke about her. Lourdes was convinced that it was best for him to forget her, to forget the whole dreadful ordeal. Why stir up bad memories? This was why whenever he looked forlorn, Lourdes kissed him on the forehead and said: "Brave boys don't cry, mi cielo."

Por supuesto, her daughter disparaged Lourdes's every effort on Eliseo's behalf. On their last phone call, Pilar went on the offensive.

"The boy belongs with his father in Cuba!"

"Imagine that you die," Lourdes countered, "and your wishes for your son are disregarded—"

"Way to make a point, Mom."

"Then Azul's father files custody to have him returned to Japan."

"That's in no way analogous."

"It's very analala—parecido!" Lourdes's worst fear was that her grandson would grow up to despise her, like Pilar did. Then whom could she call family?

"Azul doesn't know his father, or speak Japanese. He's never even been to Japan!"

"Exactly!"

"Exactly what, Mom? Eliseo has a loving, involved father who wants him home."

"A loving father would want what's best for his child!"

"Which you get to decide?"

"No, his family in Miami does!" Lourdes switched the phone from one scalding ear to the other. It was all she could do not to shout, "¡ELISEO NO SE VA!"

"But he didn't grow up with them!"

Lourdes tried a more underdog-friendly approach. "His relatives here are very nice people, gente humilde. How can you attack those poor guajiros? And Marisol is having nervous breakdowns día y noche."

"I don't care how nice, or mentally unstable, they are. They're not his father. And since when do you give a damn about 'poor guajiros'?"

"Eliseo's mother died trying to bring him to freedom!"

"She kidnapped him. Without informing his father. Can't you see how horrible that is? Oh, I forgot. You think nothing of kidnapping innocent children."

"This has nothing to do with Ivanito, and you know it!" Saving her nephew from Communist Cuba was the proudest moment of Lourdes's life. Was it any wonder Pilar desecrated it?

"It has everything to do with him!"

"As if you didn't do your part!"

"That was *after* you dumped him at the Peruvian embassy!"

Why did every conversation with her daughter feel like the one aerobics class Lourdes had taken at the yacht club? That torturous hour had left her waddling in pain for days. "The point is that Eliseo survived. Y milagrosamente."

"Jesus, Mom! You're acting out some deluded savior fantasy again!"

"El niño deserves a chance for a better life!"

"It's outrageous!"

"The real outrage will be if he doesn't get that chance!" What other Cuban mother had to put up with such falta de respeto?

Lourdes took a deep breath and calculated her next move. She couldn't risk alienating Pilar if she wanted to see her grandson again.

"¿Y cómo está Azulito?"

"He's fine, Mom. With a mother who loves him."

"What about his abuela, who also loves him?"

"What about her?"

"When will I get to see him again?"

"You can fly to California anytime you want."

The phone emitted a suspicious squeal, as if the FBI were spying on them. Rumors were flying that the government was recording the calls of pro-Eliseo factions in Miami. Everyone was under surveillance, just like in Cuba. What could you expect from President Clinton and those traitorous Democrats?

"I can't travel right now."

"Why not?"

"Because I made a promise."

"To whom?"

"To La Virgen de la Caridad del Cobre. About my mission."

"Your mission? What are you now, an astronaut for Catholicism?"

Lourdes swallowed with difficulty. She hated to beg but she was desperate. "Bring Azul to me in Miami. Por favor, I need my boy. It's been eight months! It's unfair that you keep him from me."

"Oh, please." Pilar exhaled dramatically. "Let's not go there."

Her daughter was forty-one years old but still behaved like a teenager. She had no husband or career to speak of. Teaching a class here and there, selling an incomprehensible sculpture de vez en cuando. No wonder she was chronically depressed. All Lourdes had ever wanted was for Pilar to lead a happy, normal life. Was that too much to ask?

"Let me think about it."

"¿Qué dices?" Lourdes tried to tamp down her enthusiasm. She didn't want to give her daughter any excuse to change her mind. "¿De veras?"

"I said I'd think about it."

Lourdes hung up the phone, cautiously elated. She resented having to be so careful around her daughter, picking her words like prickly pears. Would Pilar view her differently if she knew what Lourdes had suffered in the early days of the Revolution?

It was a hot July morning in 1961 when Rufino took off to buy a cow-milking machine in Havana. Two soldiers showed up at the ranch and handed Lourdes a deed that declared their property belonged to the state. She tore the deed in half and ordered them to leave. "So, the woman of the house is a fighter?" the taller soldier sneered. Lourdes tried to run past him but he pushed her to the ground while the other soldier stood guard. It didn't matter to him that she was pregnant. He raped her. Then he carved her belly with his army knife. She lost her unborn son that same night.

Pilar arrived with Azul at the Miami airport a few weeks later, saying she needed a break from work. ¿Qué trabajo? Her daughter had little to show for her so-called work. But Lourdes was thrilled to see her grandson again. How he'd grown! And what a darling boy, tall for his age (despite the meat deprivation), a half-head taller than Eliseo, though they were only a month apart in age. She was certain that the boys would get along beautifully, if given a chance. Lourdes offered to drive straight over to the famous white bungalow in Little Havana, but Pilar threatened her.

"Don't do it, Mom, or we'll get on the next plane out of here."

Lourdes glanced in the rearview mirror. Her grandson was sticking his head out the window like a puppy. "Cuídate, mi cielo, que una guagua will speed by and cut off your head." She underscored her warning with a chopping motion. "¡Fuácata!"

"What's a *guagua*?" Azul asked.

"It's the Cuban word for 'bus,'" Pilar said, then turned and hissed at Lourdes. "Could you please spare us your worst-case scenarios?"

Lourdes was seething, but pressed her lips tight. How could Azulito understand that the world was divided into opposing camps—
his mother in one, his grandmother in the other? She pulled into
the Oasis Café on Key Biscayne. Her grandson ordered pastelitos de
guayaba. It was a start, menos mal. Soon Lourdes hoped to have him
eating medianoches, lechón asado, chuletas de puerco smothered
with onions. Once her grandson got a taste of Cuban-style pork,
he'd never touch tofu again.

At the yacht club, Rufino was waiting to take them for a spin
around Biscayne Bay in his fancy new boat. "¡Ven, ven!" he boomed,
hugging Pilar and Azul so hard they nearly toppled into the water.
"I've missed you!"

"We've missed you, too, Dad." Pilar pecked him on the cheek.

Lourdes felt a pang of jealousy but managed to suppress it. She
would concentrate her efforts on Azulito.

The heat on the docks was searing. Rufino was tickled to play
el capitán, showing off his nautical gadgetry, his seafaring savvy.
He hoisted Azulito behind the boat's wheel and let him twist it
right and left. "It's only a hundred and ninety-eight nautical miles
to Cuba! Want to go with your abuelo?"

"Yeah!"

"¿Y por qué no?" Rufino laughed. "¡Aventurero eres!"

Lourdes listened impatiently to her husband's nonsense, wip-
ing her neck with a washcloth from the onboard freezer. Recently,
he'd taken a group of yacht club widows out for a joy ride. Lourdes
waited for the group's return, then promptly shoved her husband
off the dock. Ahoy, indeed.

"Por favor, mi amor, can you untie the ropes for me?" he called
out now.

Lourdes planted her hands on her hips. "Don't tell me what to
do!"

"Non ducor, duco."

"What did he say?" Pilar asked.

Lourdes was sick and tired of Rufino showing off his stupid high school Latin, too.

"But we can't go anywhere moored to the dock!" he whined.

"Oh, for Christ's sake, I'll do it," Pilar said. "C'mon, Azul. Give me a hand."

Her grandson loved getting in the thick of anything practical. He was turning into un hombrecito despite Pilar's best efforts at feminizing him. Lourdes was thrilled when she'd heard that Azul had demolished the dolls Pilar had bought for him. He was a real boy, who loved trucks and baseball, hecho y derecho like any red-blooded cubanito.

A manatee sidled up to the dock, displaying its huge, algae-encrusted head. Azul's eyes grew wide at the sight of the giant, slow-moving beast. "Is it a monster, Abuela? Will it eat us?"

"No, mi cielo, it's a sea mammal. It lives in the sea."

Pilar rolled her eyes. "Way to go with the marine biology lesson."

Lourdes decided to ignore the insult. Pilar often reverted to her adolescent self in the company of her mother. Instead Lourdes handed Azul a romaine lettuce from her canvas bag of supplies. "Pull off the leaves, corazón, and throw them to him one by one."

But Azul was so wound up that he pitched the entire head of lettuce at the manatee, bonking it between the eyes. The beast floated patiently in the turquoise waters before locating the lettuce and sucking it in all at once. Azul was transfixed.

Por supuesto, Pilar had to ruin the moment. "You know," she said, clutching her son by the waist so he wouldn't slip and fall into the water, "manatees are vegetarian."

Lourdes flared up. "Even this, you turn into something political!"

When Pilar's incredulity turned to helpless laughter, Rufino insisted that they pose for a picture. Lourdes knew what her husband was thinking: that it was rare for Pilar to find even fleeting joy in her company and he wanted to capture the moment. As they assembled for the shot, Lourdes's smile was glazed hard by self-restraint. Pilar looked bug-eyed, like a chicken spotting a fox. Only Azul appeared genuinely happy. He got to feed a manatee today. His face was beaming. Who knew that this would be the last photograph of them together?

Over the next two days Lourdes's nerves were on edge. It was exhausting trying to behave when her daughter continually provoked her. *Turn off Fox News! Turn up the thermostat! This cereal has sixty-three grams of sugar per serving!* Pilar refused to let Azul wear the American flag T-shirt Lourdes had bought for him, too. Another stab in the back! Coño, she was overeating from the stress—an entire tres leches cake, para empezar—and anxiously pacing through the night.

The Eliseo case, with its many legal flip-flops, was reaching a feverish pitch. Lourdes listened to TV and radio reports on the sly, left urgent messages for the boy's uncles, who were buckling under the strain. An apparition by La Virgen de la Caridad del Cobre in a window of the Flagler Street branch of Northern Trust Bank incited a frenzied pilgrimage, redoubling Lourdes's resolve, and gave birth to the rallying cry "La Virgen is on our side!"

When word came down from the State Department that the boy's father, José Miguel, was en route to Washington, DC, everyone expected him to defect the instant he set foot on U.S. soil. Who in their right mind would return to Cuba by choice? Then news broke that the Justice Department—headed by esa gorgona U.S. Attorney General Janet Reno—planned to return Eliseo to his father. Lourdes was incensed. Why should she forgo the mission of a lifetime just because her daughter objected?

When Pilar took off for her morning walk on the beach, Lourdes sprang into action. It was time to show her grandson what it meant to stand up for one's principles.

"¡Apúrate, mi cielo!" Lourdes stuffed his backpack with fruit juice boxes, then hustled him down to the garage and into her lavender Jaguar.

Lourdes blasted Radio Mambí, swigging espresso from a jumbo thermos and issuing orders to Azul during the commercial breaks: *Don't talk to anyone with a microphone, ¿me oyes? . . . All you need to say is this: "¡ELISEO NO SE VA!" Can you do that? . . . Let me hear you, Azulito! . . . LOUDER, mi cielo! . . . Así, perfecto. ¡Qué inteligente eres! . . . Y corazón, let's keep this little adventure to ourselves, okay?*

It was drizzling when a highly caffeinated Lourdes and her grandson arrived at the Gonzálezes' white bungalow. Journalists swarmed the car, cameras flashing, clamoring for a quote. "Who's the kid?" a CNN reporter shouted, but Lourdes pushed past him. Eliseo's uncles were in the yard, visibly drunk. Marisol, as usual, was having another breakdown for the cameras. A crowd was gathering and spilling down the side streets. Lourdes took Azul to play with Eliseo inside the house. No doubt her boys would get along like brothers. Hadn't La Virgen promised her as much?

Back outside, she grabbed a bullhorn.

"¡ELISEO NO SE VA!" Lourdes thundered.

"¡ELISEO NO SE VA!" the mob thundered back.

As they marched toward Calle Ocho, all of Little Havana turned out for the protest. They banged pots and pans, shook maracas and chekeres, scraped güiros, rang cowbells, blew whistles into a deafening clangor. A few held up portraits of Cuba's political prisoners side by side with el polaco Pope John Paul II. Street vendors hawked Eliseo buttons, Cuban flags, paletas de coco, chicharrones, cups of pineapple chunks, and laminated prayer cards for La Virgen de la Caridad del Cobre.

"¡ABAJO EL TIRANO! ¡ABAJO CLINTON!"

Eliseo was their boy now, representing everyone and everything the Cuban Revolution had stolen from them. What was nostalgia except the last refuge of those who'd lost their worlds? To hand

Eliseo back to El Líder would be the worst betrayal imaginable—to their history, their suffering, their sacrifices. Lourdes had lost one boy to the Revolution; she refused to surrender another.

"¡LIBERTAD! ¡LIBERTAD!"

The protesters trudged toward the Caballero Rivero cemetery, where many of the Bay of Pigs veterans had been laid to rest. The lead marchers tried to hoist Lourdes onto their shoulders but they lost their grip and she pitched forward onto the grave of Desi Arnaz's father, a former mayor of Santiago de Cuba. As she was dusting herself off, a phalanx of policemen arrived on horseback and charged their peaceful demonstration like the cavalry.

"¡A LOS FRENTES DE BATALLA!" Lourdes commanded. Later, it would become known as *el grito que levantó a los muertos*, the cry that woke the dead. Gone was any pretense of assimilation. The rift between Cuban exiles and their adopted country was exposed—an open, festering wound for all to see.

Protesters pelted the cops with pork rinds and pineapple chunks, then rushed to form a human chain, attempting to block them and their horses from advancing into the cemetery. With some difficulty the police broke through their ranks and chased the demonstrators around tombstones and mausoleums, deployed batons and choke holds against the most disorderly. They sent funeral wreaths flying, stomped on flower arrangements, cracked granite memorial plaques.

A panting Lourdes made an uphill run for it and took shelter in the cremation garden. "¡TRAIDORES!" she snarled when a pair of cops cornered her against the columbarium of a Peruvian pop singer.

"Put your hands up!" the rookie demanded, brandishing a nightstick.

When he tried to handcuff her, Lourdes bit his ear and walloped his partner with her bullhorn. No sooner did she break free than she tripped on the roots of a banyan tree and tumbled thirty yards downhill.

Waves of reinforcements arrived in squad cars and on motorcycles. They sprayed tear gas to disperse the mob, who staggered off—coughing, and cursing, and vowing revenge. Lourdes made a last stand on the grave of Anastasio Somoza, the Nicaraguan dictator, staring down a row of heavily armed police. Eyewitnesses swore that Lourdes Puente resisted arrest como una fiera, screaming, "LA VIRGEN IS ON OUR SIDE!" Overpowered at last, she was hauled away with dozens of other freedom fighters.

In the mayhem nobody noticed the boy slurping a fruit juice box on the periphery of the violence, right outside the cemetery gates. He was trampled by the fleeing protesters and knocked unconscious. An auto mechanic noticed the boy and carried him to his roadside emergency truck. Then he drove him to Jackson Memorial Hospital. Many in the exile community proclaimed six-year-old Azul Puente-Tanaka as the youngest hero of that day's historical insurrection.

Unfortunately, the boy's mother didn't see it that way.

2

Luz and Milagro Villaverde

Miami

I was the talker of the two—a fast talker, even for a cubana—but Milagro always understood what was going down. It was her secret power. We were a double helix, impossible to separate. My sister was born twelve minutes after me, waiting for the all clear. On the surface I was tougher, hotheaded, a fighter. But Milagro's good sense won out every time. How did anyone manage without a twin?

After our brother was born, Mamá began grooming him to be her little sycophant. We rallied around Ivanito, tried to enlist him against her. We told him that if he didn't side with us, he would end up crazy like her. But nothing could persuade him that she wasn't a saint. Not even after she tried to poison them both when he was a kid. Ultimately, she succeeded in killing herself, but dying only reinforced her holiness in his eyes.

Our brother was convinced that we were united against him, against his happiness with Mamá. But he never saw what we saw: Mamá pouring a pan of hot cooking oil on our sleeping father, or filling Milagro's and my birthday piñata with raw eggs. Ivanito ended up leaving Cuba years before we did. Tía Lourdes kidnapped him at the start of the Mariel exodus. Our cousin Pilar was in on it, too. Abuela Celia never forgave them. We haven't seen him since.

Milagro and I studied nautical engineering in Guantánamo,

then worked in Havana's port fixing the engines of international oil tankers. The money was good—better than what brain surgeons make—on account of our foreign-currency bonuses. Eventually, Papi convinced us to join him in Miami. It took us eleven months to build a boat sturdy enough to cross the Straits of Florida. Thousands of balseros tried every year, only to end up as shark bait. Most couldn't navigate their way out of a puddle.

Our father was waiting for us, like he'd promised. What we didn't know was that he'd also married a gringa to fast-track his citizenship papers. He didn't abandon us, not right away. First, he got us jobs bagging groceries at a Publix in Hialeah. Later, Tía Lourdes hired us to fix our uncle's boat, which, given our skills, led to a lot more work.

Today, Papi was supposed to meet Milagro and me for lunch at Versailles, a Cuban cafetería in Little Havana—ridiculous, with wall-to-wall mirrors, tacky chandeliers, and Heimlich maneuver posters in Spanish (you'd choke to death if you spoke only English). My sister and I sat next to a table of matrons in pastel suits and pearl necklaces, enjoying their Pollo Imperial specials.

Calle Ocho was a stretch of second-rate stores and restaurants flash-frozen in the sixties. It had nothing of the real Havana's colonial majesty, even in ruins. The older exiles—self-avowed Bay of Pigs veterans to the last—bolted back cafecitos so sweet it tightened their dentures. They bragged about their fincas back home, too. Créame, if those ranches actually existed, Cuba would be the size of Brazil.

Anyway, the last time we saw Papi was the week before Christmas—and he cut short our visit. Since then he'd broken a half-dozen dates with us, always with the same excuse: family obligations. Coño, didn't we count as family? Papi had a son from his new marriage and talked about him like he walked on water. Maybe all he ever wanted was a boy he could teach to become a man, who'd worship him, no questions asked.

Our clients liked to tell us how lucky we were to be living in Miami, away from the hellhole that was Communist Cuba. What did they really care about our grease-monkey opinions? The truth was that it was complicated for us—and got more complicated the longer we stayed. What the exiles here expected was irrefutable agreement. If we didn't agree with them, we became the enemy. With us or against us, just like la revolución.

A look between Milagro and me—our usual telepathy—meant Papi wasn't going to show up. Maybe he was never going to show up. Maybe he'd just keep us in limbo with his half promises, with the sad reality of our fractured family, multiplied a thousand times by the cheap-ass mirrors at Versailles. We scanned the menu and ordered identical lunches: palomilla steaks with papitas fritas. Y así se quedó la cosa.

3

Pilar Puente

Miami to Berlin

So, just like that, we left Miami and decamped for Berlin, with one-way tickets. Because Ivanito was there. Because its art scene was happening. Because so many of my musical heroes had found inspiration there: David Bowie, U2, Iggy Pop. Maybe I'd get a little inspiration, too. What the hell did I have to lose? My career was dead, my love life nonexistent, and my mother certifiably unhinged. In short, a big hot bowl of nothing.

It wasn't that difficult to leave L.A. I took Azul out of school, sublet my leaky house and studio to friends, and took off with our week's worth of clothes. Plus I had some money left over from a grant that would last us a few months. At least, I told myself, I wasn't too old to be spontaneous.

My son was sleeping next to me in the back of the plane. As I re-checked the bandages on his head, I grew enraged all over again. Even after Azul ended up in the emergency room, having been stomped on by the mob my mother had been leading, she refused to acknowledge any wrongdoing. Mom swore she'd left Azul playing with Eliseo, against my express wishes. But instead of apologizing, she focused on the indignity of her arrest, her millisecond of jail time, and her latest Virgin-approved calling to run for mayor of Miami-Dade County.

I left a message on Ivanito's answering machine about our impending arrival in Berlin. I didn't think he'd mind. My cousin and I had been super tight in the eighties. When he was still in high school, I let him join my all-girl punk band, Autopsy, on the condition that he perform in drag. Believe me, I didn't have to ask twice. Ivanito couldn't sing worth shit—an asset in punk—but the incongruity of his rarefied androgyny presiding over our trio of sweating, hard-playing feminists was magic.

His stage name? Miss Violet Water. Perfect for a Cuban mami's boy.

I never actually got to meet his mother, Tía Felicia, who died shortly before my one trip to Cuba. There were lots of stories about her. By all accounts, she was a handful. An avenging hairdresser. An outspoken malcontent of the Revolution. A loving but erratic mother. A voracious romantic (she'd had dozens of lovers and three husbands, two of whom she'd allegedly killed). And barking mad. Everyone swore she was genetically prone to excess. Poor Ivanito loved her as desperately as his twin sisters hated her.

Miss Violet Water became a downtown sensation and catapulted Autopsy to the peak of its popularity. We played the best, grungiest clubs: CBGB's, the Mudd Club (before it closed), A7, the Pyramid Club, Club 82. I swaggered around with my white Fender Precision bass like it was the world's biggest dick. Apparently, I had the personality to match. Whenever Ivanito got depressed or homesick for Cuba, we headed to Veselka in the East Village. It took two bowls of borscht and a heap of blinis to cheer him up.

Our band broke up just as punk was imploding. Nothing left but a black hole stuffed with assholes, ideologues, codifications, mainstreaming, commercialism, confusion, and sorrow. Big-time sorrow. Most of us who'd been part of the scene free-floated for a few years, lost and unmoored, scattering to the winds. I waited tables at the Empire Diner for a while (worst job ever), then went off to art grad school in Los Angeles. The city seemed like an endless suburban wasteland to me. Nothing open past ten o'clock except for Canter's Deli, where a few ad hoc punks gathered. I stopped playing bass altogether.

Ivanito flew off to perfect his Russian in Moscow, where he witnessed the unraveling of the Soviet Union. I used to mail him abstract acrylics on postcards with lyrics from our old Autopsy songs—"Fibrillation," "Body Cavities," "Bedside Scammer" (*Get out of here with your bedside manner / Leave me alone you dirtbag scammer . . .*). Ivanito told me he saved the postcards, convinced they'd be worth a fortune someday. Ha! All this was to say that we'd kept track of each other despite our lives radically diverging. My cousin became a hotshot translator in Berlin and I . . . well, I was a failed artist. There, I said it.

The stewardess rolled by with a cart loaded with boxes of suspect food: processed cheese, luncheon meats, chemical crackers, clusters of desiccated grapes. I ordered an instant hot chocolate for Azul, who'd been mumbling pro-Eliseo chants in his sleep (Fuuck!).

"How much longer, Mom?"

"About eight hours."

"Isn't that, like, all day?"

"Mostly all night."

"Then we get there?"

"Then we change planes." I wiped a chocolate stain off his chin with my thumb.

"How much longer after that?"

"A few hours."

"What's 'a few'?"

My comforts as a mother were two: that Azul could say whatever he wanted to me without fear; and that he wasn't ashamed of me— not yet, anyway.

"Let's say another four hours, including time to change planes."

Azul gnawed on his cheese. "Do you speak German?"

"Uh, not so well. I took a class in college but dropped out."

"You dropped out of school?"

"No, not school. I dropped out of a class."

"Can I do that, too?"

"Azul, you're in first grade. What could you possibly want to drop out of?"

"Singing. It's stupid."

"You don't like to sing?"

"Not with the other kids. We sound like . . ."

"Like what?"

"Like really bad." He stared out at the wilderness that was thirty thousand feet below.

"Are we moving?"

"Yep."

"It doesn't look like it. How fast are we going?"

"About five hundred miles per hour."

"Wow. But why can't we tell?"

"Because there's nothing around to show us how fast we're going." Like the trajectories of everyone else's exploding art careers, I wanted to say, but kept my mouth shut.

"What about the clouds?"

"They look stationary, though they're not." I smoothed his hair and gave him a kiss. "Aren't you tired?"

"No." He snuggled against me and conked out a minute later.

I thought about the long history of one-way tickets in my family. My parents emigrating from Havana to Miami before heading north to New York. Me with my one-way bus ticket to Florida when I was thirteen, then much later another bus to Los Angeles. But Ivanito had far and away the most one-way tickets of all: from Havana to Lima; Lima to Mexico City (where Mom picked him up, proffering sticky buns); Mexico City to New York; New York to Moscow; and, last, a one-way train ticket from Moscow to Berlin.

The stewardess distributed German newspapers, including a tabloid with a front-page story about, as far as my German would let me discern, a polar bear who'd disappeared from the Berlin Zoo with its keeper. Was my cousin following this? Back in New York, Ivanito used to keep clippings about missing people: the octogenarian last spotted buying lingerie at Macy's; a nine-year-old boy who'd vanished on his four-block walk home from school; pet alligators lost to the city's sewer system.

Did Ivanito consider himself a missing person? After all, he'd left Cuba without warning. My mother was responsible. She'd kidnapped him in the middle of the night and dumped him at the Peruvian embassy in Havana just as the Mariel exodus was exploding. She considered this her most successful effort as a one-woman bulwark against Communism. The next morning, I tracked Ivanito down on the embassy grounds. He begged me to let him leave the country.

What could I do? I lied to Abuela Celia, told her I couldn't find him. But she knew the truth.

As we flew across the Atlantic, I grew uneasy. Was it a mistake to parachute into my cousin's life without warning? Did he remember our times together differently? Less generously? I was too wired to sleep so I turned up my MP3 player and listened to U2's *Achtung Baby* album. The opening song, "Zoo Station," was a sonic assault. I was itching to play the bass part, its groove steady amid the gorgeous distortion. *Time is a train / Makes the future the past . . .*

"Do you think they ran away together?" Azul asked me after I told him the news about the missing polar bear. "Was it consensual?"

Shit, I taught him that word and now he was using it at every turn. "I'm not sure."

"Are they getting married?" Azul tapped his left ear, a sign of distress.

His question startled me. Was he thinking about his father and me *not* being married? Or that he didn't have a father, except theoretically, far away in Japan? To him, Haru Tanaka was just a name, a photo of some old Asian guy who was supposed to be his dad. How would he have a clue about the unflinching assurance with which Haru commanded a room? Or his weakness for horse racing and fancy silk socks? Or the sufferings he'd endured as a starving boy in post–World War II Yokohama? How casually bad service in the U.S. infuriated him?

"They can't get married," I said.

"Why not?"

"Only people get married." Did Azul sense my heartbreak? The before and after that had divided my life? Before he came along, of course.

"Don't birds mate for life?"

"True. But a bird can't marry a leopard."

"But they could be friends, right?"

"I guess so." My answer seemed to satisfy him, for the moment.

INTERLUDE:
PILAR'S PHOTOS

Image #3: 1965

It's dusk. The light sifts over our house, a refurbished warehouse in Brooklyn. I'm scowling at the camera as Mom twists my arm behind my back. There's a laundry basket filled with dirty clothes at my feet. I'm six years old and wearing the blue-apples shirt I love. The minute I saw those blue apples—not red, like they're supposed to be—I wanted them. They became the emblem of my first great escape.

Earlier that day, an old college friend of my parents came with us to Sunken Meadow Beach. I don't remember his name—let's call him Hernando de Soto—only that he told me he had a daughter my age back in Cuba. Her name was Sarita. I took an instant liking to Hernando, a rarity for me. As a baby I'd glowered at everyone, made my nannies' hair fall out with my stares. They called me "brujita" and wore kerchiefs to cover their bald patches. This embarrassed my mother, who accused me of undermining her maternal image.

At the beach Hernando taught me how to float on my back, bought me a Creamsicle, rubbed sunscreen on the tops of my ears so they wouldn't burn. He grew sad when he talked about Sarita and said he prayed every night for her to come live with him in Washington Heights. "The Communists," he complained bitterly, "have turned her mother's head around."

I heard the word *Communist* a lot when I was growing up. To be a Communist was the most mortal of mortal sins. But before I was out of grade school Mom started calling me a Communist, too—for skipping Sunday Mass, or flushing my broccoli down the toilet.

As we were packing up at the beach to go home, Hernando asked: "Pilarcita, do you want to come home with me instead of your parents?"

"Yes!" I cried without a second's hesitation.

Everybody laughed, thinking it was a joke, but it wasn't a joke to me.

"Ay, she doesn't mean it!" Mom insisted. "Say you don't mean it, mi cielo."

"I do mean it," I said. "Yes!" I repeated, louder this time.

A strained silence hung over the station wagon as we drove back to Brooklyn. We dropped off Hernando at the Borough Hall subway station without so much as a good-bye. When I tried to bolt, Mom gripped my elbow.

"Lo siento, Pilarcita," Hernando said, rescinding his offer. "Your parents love you very much and want to keep you."

"But you promised!" I shouted as he hurried down the steps to catch his train.

When we got home Mom pulled my dirty clothes out of the hamper and flung them into a laundry basket. I was scared, and excited. Would I really get to leave? Would Hernando return to pick me up? I changed into my blue-apples shirt, clipped a barrette in my hair, and double-tied my shoelaces. I was ready to go.

Mom thrust the smelly basket at me. "Lárgate de aquí."

I glanced at my father, who was his usual passive self, then headed out the door with the dirty clothes. An ice cream truck drove by slowly, chiming its bell. Sparrows twittered on the telephone lines. Other mothers called their kids in for supper. My life had changed drastically but the world stayed exactly the same. How was that possible?

When I heard a cargo ship blow its horn, I walked toward the East River, toward the promise of far away. Maybe I could talk my way onto a steamer bound for Cuba? Reunite with Abuela Celia? Track down Sarita and bring her home to her father? We could become stepsisters and live happily ever after, not like those mean stepsisters in the Cinderella story.

Suddenly, I heard my mother shouting my name, the second syllable more of a howl. A part of me wanted to hide but another part was too frightened to do that. I stopped and waited for her to find me. Mom hugged me hard, then slapped me equally hard. I refused to cry. I knew how to be una ingrata.

She dragged me home and ordered Dad to get out the Polaroid camera and snap our picture—to remember the day I'd disgraced myself, disgraced us both.

Image #4: 1973

This isn't a regular photograph but a square of my face in a document that resembles a passport but isn't one. It's a re-entry permit issued by the U.S. Department of Justice in 1973. My mother found it when she was rummaging through her storage boxes.

> Pursuant to the provision of Section 223 of the Immigration and Nationality Act, this permit is issued to the person named herein, an alien previously lawfully admitted to the United States for permanent residence, to reenter the United States as a special immigrant if otherwise admissible.

Talk about a Cold War relic. The permit was issued to me on June 26, 1973, when I was fourteen, and it expired on the same day a year later. My long hair is parted down the middle and my height is recorded as five feet, zero inches, my eyes as hazel. I don't remember ever having this document in my possession—or being so short, for that matter. I grew eight inches by the time I graduated high school.

> This document is not valid for return to the United States after a temporary absence which involves travel to, in or through any of the following countries unless the restriction is specifically waived with regard to any such country or countries by indorsement [*sic*] hereon:

Communist portions of:

~~Albania~~	~~China~~
Cuba	Korea
~~Outer Mongolia~~	Viet-Nam

On the permit, Albania, China, and Outer Mongolia are crossed out with a black marker. I know now that the Chinese Cultural Revolution had been catastrophically under way but I'm still clueless about what was going on in Albania or Outer Mongolia. Why were they crossed out? Cuba, Korea, and Vietnam were all countries where the U.S. had sent troops—and, in the case of Vietnam, were still fighting.

"Why did I need this permit?" I asked my mother, but got no response.

Did she apply for it after I ran away in 1972, intent on returning to Cuba to see Abuela Celia? To Mom's shock, I'd hopped aboard a Greyhound bus and gotten as far as Miami before my father's relatives dispatched me back to Brooklyn. Maybe she planned to make good on her promise to ship me overseas to study, far from the radical elements destabilizing the country? I remember how apoplectic she got over my mustard-colored bell-bottoms—a hip-hugging pair that I wore with peasant blouses, sandals (or bare feet), and love beads. Proof positive to her of my budding Communism.

But I don't remember having this picture taken. Or becoming an

American citizen three years later, though my papers state that the swearing-in ceremony took place at the federal courthouse in downtown Brooklyn, a stone's throw from my mother's second Yankee Doodle Bakery. It was there that I would paint a mural of the Statue of Liberty with a safety pin through her nose—inspired, of course, by the Sex Pistols' "God Save the Queen" single.

Why can I recall certain details of my past so specifically yet forget hulking swaths of others? Is that how memory works? Do we pick and choose what we need to survive? I look at this photo—my unflinching gaze, the defiant posture—and think I'm still that fourteen-year-old girl saying: *Go ahead, try me.*

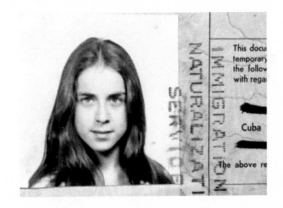

GRANADA–HAVANA

Celia del Pino

In which the lovers meet in Granada after sixty-six years . . .

Celia spotted him first. He was wearing a bone-colored suit and leaning loosely on his cane as if it were decorative, a bit of foppery. A spray of red carnations floated luminously from his grasp. Gustavo was bald and elegant but didn't remotely resemble the man she remembered. His left eye looked milky, too—a cataract? Celia waited, watching him, as her past and present converged. Gustavo continued to scan the arriving passengers and finally settled on her. His expression flagged, almost imperceptibly, but his eyes remained joyful. Celia's fitted green dress was cinched at the waist but she felt no less a relic.

Verde que te quiero verde.

How long had she dreamed of this moment? But in her dream she and Gustavo were the same ages they'd been in 1934—supple-skinned, indefatigable, lovesick. Youth was an immortal god and they had been gods together. Yet this old man didn't displease Celia, either. His face was baby-smooth, almost pearlescent, and she had to stop herself from stroking his cheek.

"Mi amor." Gustavo dropped his cane with a clatter and moved toward her, arms wide, carnations drooping. His gait was confident, though lurching. He stood before Celia, unblinking as a child, searching for who she'd once been inside of who she was now. He cupped her chin with a papery hand, his fingers gnarled, knuckles shining, as if he'd polished them for the occasion. "You haven't changed a bit."

Then Gustavo leaned toward her with lips redolent of eucalyptus and kissed Celia full on the mouth—the tip of his tongue skirting hers—oblivious to the sea of rushing, irritable travelers around them.

Verde viento. Verdes ramas.

"So, we begin with a lie?" Celia was startled yet quietly delighted.

Gustavo's kiss registered seismically in her body, in its crevices and hidden rivers. Who knew she was still capable of such heat? It always began with the tongue, she thought, that most miraculous of muscles. A part of her didn't want to waste another minute in small talk, preferring to lock themselves up in a hotel room for four more days. That would add up to eight days of bliss in one lifetime. How many people could claim even that?

"It's no lie," Gustavo said simply, glancing at the carnations now scattered on the faux marble floor. His teeth were unnaturally white. Were they dentures? Would he need to remove them at night, brush them like a precious accessory, drop them in a glass fizzing with cleaning tablets? What other grisly details awaited them?

What they needed, urgently, was an armoire in which to store all the telltale signs of old age: joint ointments and reading glasses, incontinence pads, blood pressure medications, orthopedic inserts, enemas, antacids, compression socks. There were no lasting remedies for their beleaguered bodies—unruly sags and pouches, arthritic creaks and drooping declivities, acres of wrinkles, meshwork of varicose veins. Only moonlight and artful camouflage could save them.

Celia ignored the pain in her neck from the immobilizing flights. Her ankles were swollen, her stomach acidic, and cold air had settled in her knees. She'd hardly slept, only a sporadic dozing that left her frazzled. At a lingerie boutique at the Madrid airport, where Celia caught a connecting flight to Granada, she'd splurged on a lacy red push-up bra with matching panties. If that wasn't optimism, what was? The checkout clerk had curiously reviewed her selections but Celia refused to submit to any transgenerational camaraderie.

Verde que te quiero verde.

"No?" Gustavo asked.

"No, what?"

"You're shaking your head." He looked bemused but with a hint of worry.

"I was just thinking of other things."

"I stand before you after sixty-six years—and you're *distracted*? I must look like hell!"

Celia laughed. They held each other's gaze for a long moment, ignoring the loudspeakers announcing flights to Marrakesh, Nairobi, São Paulo, Calcutta. On her deathbed, Gustavo's incurably jealous wife had made him swear that he wouldn't contact Celia again. But death, as everyone knew, broke every promise.

Bajo la luna gitana . . .

"Let's both enjoy our beautiful lies," Celia said, her flirtation surfacing. "And promise each other this: that in the time we have left, we'll always choose a good story over the truth. Unless the truth is the better story."

"But how will we know the difference?"

"We won't. That's what I'm telling you." Coño, was she going to have to explain everything to him?

"Telling me what?" Gustavo insisted.

"¿Qué cosa?" Celia turned her head, the better to hear him. Her left ear felt clogged, as if stuffed with cotton, a residual from the ear-popping flights. She felt a headache coming on, too. Nothing a cafecito with extra sugar wouldn't fix.

"About truth!"

"Ay, that it doesn't matter!" The last thing Celia wanted was to rehash the past. ¿Qué más da? She was here in Granada, wasn't she?

Their memories were crumbs, subject to birds, to breezes. They had no time to grow old all over again. But a little flamenco? A gypsy moon? A night to sing, to dance, to fling themselves back into the heart of love?

Verde carne, pelo verde . . .

"I want you to believe everything I tell you." Gustavo was resolute. He slipped a pair of wire-rimmed glasses from his jacket and put them on. His eyes grew enormous behind the lenses, like a tree frog's, the better to track her with.

"I'll believe everything you tell me, true or not." Celia was impatient to stop this nonsense before it went any further. There was no time to waste. After the tremendous effort to get here, she feared losing her nerve—and the momentum of that first kiss.

"And I need you to forgive me."

"How Catholic of you," Celia said brusquely. "How far is the Alhambra from here?"

"I'm serious, Celia."

"How far?"

"Not too far. But I'm not ready for us to be tourists yet!"

"I'm here. Isn't that forgiveness enough?"

"It might just be curiosity."

"I've traveled a long way." Celia was hungry and cranky and her head throbbed from the lack of caffeine. "And in circles, it seems."

"Progress is always circular."

Con ojos de fría plata.

Celia didn't remember Gustavo ever being this stubbornly garrulous. It was not an appealing feature.

"You know the most crucial thing I learned when I traveled?" Gustavo droned on.

Maybe if she remained silent, if they both remained silent, if their mouths were no longer diverted by the impositions of language, their bodies would take the lead.

"That I don't exist."

"No entiendo," she said.

"Traveling is a liminal space, suspended in time. Like us."

"But I exist," Celia shot back. "I've never stopped existing."

This wasn't getting off to an auspicious start. If her visit with Gustavo was a fracaso, she would devote her trip to the memory of García Lorca, join the pilgrims who hunted for his unmarked grave in the foothills of the Sierra Nevada, strewing armloads of lilies in his name. What else could she do? She'd come this far, and returning home was not an option.

Verde que te quiero verde.

"I have something to show you." Gustavo pulled a Minifex camera from his vest pocket, the very one Celia had sold him at El Encanto department store in 1934. "I stumbled across it last year. I took it as a sign."

Celia wondered if the camera had served its purpose. Had Gustavo secretly documented the atrocities of the Spanish Civil War through the peephole in his overcoat? Had he succeeded in bringing justice to any of the war's victims? Or, as Gustavo hinted, had he suffered on account of his deeds, been thrown in jail, tortured? Was this minuscule camera—and, by extension, Celia—responsible for his limp, for his oddly angled elbow, broken by a Falangist's club? Gustavo seemed eager to share every gruesome detail of his ordeals, whether Celia wanted to hear them or not.

"Sometimes I lose track of what's most important," he continued with regret. "And I forget what I should remember." He held up the camera and, smiling, took her picture.

For a moment Celia was grateful—relieved!—that Gustavo had abandoned her when he did. At least they'd avoided the love-suffocating rituals of conjugality. These days Celia wasn't the least bit interested in polite discourse, or suffering tedium, or pretending to ignore what annoyed her. She wanted what she wanted and refused to apologize for the wanting. At her age, didn't she deserve that much?

"I need a cafecito first." Celia balanced her purse on her left arm and took Gustavo's good elbow with her right. "Then we'll jump off a cliff together."

Herminia Delgado

Havana

When an official at the Guantánamo naval base called out my name, I hoped to leave Cuba at last. Instead I was loaded onto an army truck and brought to this women's prison outside Havana. My neighbor Gladys had been caught red-handed with my birdcages in Pinar del Río and caved under police questioning. It didn't surprise me. Survival often went hand in hand with betrayal. My sentence? Four months for trafficking in a threatened species.

The judge said she was being lenient on me because of a reference letter from Celia del Pino in my files attesting to my good standing in the community. Good standing? What the hell else had I done except sacrifice for the Revolution? Could I have sacrificed any more than my own son, que descanse en paz? How I wished I'd been arrested for something worthwhile, like burning down El Capitolio!

Hour after hour I stared through the bars of my cell at the sky, praying and watching for a sign. But only random thunderclouds replied. It was as if the orishas had forgotten me, forgotten everyone. Out of earshot of the other prisoners, I beseeched Felica: "Ayúdame, chica. I don't have forever to wait like you!"

My fellow inmates were thieves, prostitutes, malcontents, black marketeers, dissidents of all stripes. In short, ordinary citizens like me. Our side jobs kept hunger at bay, enabled us to survive. Look at me. Sixty years old and forced into illegitimate work. Prostitution was, by far, the biggest moneymaker on the island. The jineteras slept with tourists surging to Cuba for bargain sex. Even the government was cashing in, running motels that rented by the hour. Hoy en día, who could tell a nurse from a hooker?

Everything was for sale inside, too: rum, sex, tamales, drugs, cigars, de todo. But the hardest thing to get? Soap. If you traded sex for a nub of soap, nobody would judge you. Cubanos suffered—and were insufferable—without it. Mariza, our resident dealer, had a sister who worked as a housekeeper at the Hotel Nacional. Those two made a killing supplying the fragrant jaboncitos that were our only hope against the filth.

Each day brought more violent drama here. This morning, una fiera from Sancti Spíritus attacked a cellmate over her pet cricket. The chirping was driving la fiera crazy so she smashed the bicho's cage and ate it alive just to shut it up. Worse than her was the poet with rings in her nose who recited her nonsense day and night, inviting sporadic beatings.

At night we pooled our cigarettes to rent the antiquated black-and-white TV from El Baboso, the guard who came on duty at six o'clock. The Argentine telenovela *Vivir y Morir en Las Pampas* was everyone's favorite. How we rooted for Valentina Godoy, the evil mother-in-law! Her murders and double-crossings made us all feel innocent as baby chicks.

Nobody had any idea that I was a santera. Usually I'd offer to listen to people's troubles, try to lift their spirits, arrange trabajitos. You'd be surprised what you could do with a sliver of yam, or a swatch of cotton. But who had any ánimo left? The Revolution might have banished our religion in the early years but these days it charged tourists thousands of dollars for santería initiations done by charlatans. Descarados.

It was only a matter of time before the orishas took their revenge.

BERLIN

Ivanito Villaverde

Berlin

His cousins blew in to Berlin toward the end of a very rainy April. If it wasn't for the drama of blooming lavender bushes everywhere, the city would've looked flat and featureless under the overcast skies. Steady streams of bicyclists pedaled down the avenues, identical in their sensible raincoats, front baskets wrapped in plastic. It was unsettling to consider Berlin from a stranger's perspective, though Pilar was hardly a stranger.

Yet the moment Ivanito saw Azul, a flood of tenderness over-whelmed him. He embraced the boy as if he were his own six-year-old self. Azul stared up at him, enthralled and blinking, shielding his eyes with a limp salute. "Hey, what's that on your head?" he demanded. Pilar chastised him for being rude but Ivanito rejoiced. Azul could see his halo! And he took it in stride, too, like any other of Ivanito's features—the mole on his cheek, or his shoulder-length hair, or his propensity for cross-dressing.

Today, they were visiting the Zoologischer Garten for the third time in as many weeks. Nature was strutting her stuff, every blossom sprouting on cue. Daffodils lined the walkways and the flowering linden trees sweetened the air with their honey-lemon scent. Ivanito and Azul entered the zoo, hands clasped, swinging their arms to the rhythm of an old Cuban tongue twister: *Tres tristes tigres tragaban trigo en un trigal.*

"Can we see the Siberian tiger again, Tío?" Azul begged, pulling on his sleeve.

Tío was the term of address they'd settled on, though they were technically first cousins once removed. Azul was Ivanito's nephew and Ivanito was Azul's uncle except when he was his aunt, at which times Azul called her Tía Ivanita. A flood of supplemental endearments and diminutives had ensued. *Conejito,* "Little Rabbit," was a favorite.

Out of the blue, Pilar insisted to Ivanito that they all speak Spanish. Why? To practice it in Germany? She said that his Spanish sounded sanitized and cosmopolitan, weirdly unfamiliar. Por favor. Why was losing his Cuban accent tantamount to cultural betrayal? Pilar's Spanish was hardly a paragon, what with its practically non-existent subjunctive. She sounded as blunt as a Havana street tough: switchblade syllables; a broken pipe's consonantal thud. Had this come from her mother?

Ivanito snuck an assessing glance at his cousin. Pilar had put on quite a few pounds since their punk days and her hair was the washed-out color of weak tea. She looked older than her forty-one years in every way except how she dressed, sloppy as a teenager. (Those sneakers had to go!) Until she'd arrived, his memory of her was frozen in time—jet-black Mohawk; eyebrow piercings (no trace of them now); her I-don't-give-a-fuck attitude.

From what Ivanito could tell, she was stuck in that same punk mindset, rattling on about everything they'd lost, how there'd been nothing as remotely exciting since. But that had been Pilar's world, not his. When would she understand that he'd moved on?

He was heartened, at least, by their matching scorpion tattoos, vestiges of their hazy summer nights in the formerly bombed-out squalor of the Lower East Side. They'd looked out for each other then, nicknamed themselves Los Gansos, like the fierce geese that used to guard the courtyards of Old Havana. Would they ever find that solidarity again?

A group of kids invited Azul to kick a soccer ball around in a patch of grass. He was as natural an extrovert as they came—a contrast to his antisocial mother—and ran off to play. A few boys shouted in Russian, others in German and Turkish. His nephew was picking up a smattering of all three languages in the playgrounds of Berlin. It was easy for him, as it'd been for Ivanito. Each new language was a territory to conquer, another place to stand.

The halo was drilling into Ivanito's skull, as if his mother were tightening invisible screws to secure it in place. When had her love turned so despotic? Or had it been like this all along? A tremor seized his neck muscles. It was only a matter of time, he thought glumly, before the fucking thing broke his neck. Then he would be all hers. Again.

"She's back," he whispered to Pilar.

"The missing polar bear?"

"No, my mother."

"Uh, I don't understand."

"From the dead."

Pilar's breathing slowed. "You're saying that your long-deceased mother is back?"

"Correct."

"Back? Like, in your dreams back?"

"Like *back* back."

"Haunting you back?"

"I guess you could say that." Ivanito waved at Azul, who was playing goalie for the scrappy Russian team. "And she still reeks of that cheap gardenia perfume."

"No shit." Pilar let out an empathic whistle.

"Wait. You believe me?"

"Of course I believe you."

"That's insane."

"More insane than your mother returning from the dead?"

Ivanito dabbed at his eyes, which were running with mascara. Gratitude was closing off his throat like a wad of cotton. Nothing he could think to say seemed adequate. He wanted to collapse into Pilar's arms like he had during his first lonely months in New York. She'd listened to him then, shown him around, co-strategized on outmaneuvering Tía Lourdes.

Without Pilar, he would've been hopelessly lost.

"What does she want? Has she said?"

"She's pulling me toward her."

"Pulling you where?"

Ivanito wanted to say "to the afterlife," but he wasn't certain anymore. Mami hadn't shown up in more than two months. The strain of *not* knowing when she might return was taking a toll on him. The tension had become unbearable.

"Have you talked to anyone about this?"

"You mean a shrink?" Ivanito shrugged. "And end up in a loony bin out in the German countryside somewhere?"

The skies were patchy with livid clouds. From the far side of the zoo, an Asian elephant trumpeted its discontent. During World War II, the zoo had been firebombed multiple times. Ivanito had recurring flashbacks of the carnage, as if he'd witnessed it himself. Tortoises and crocodiles boiled alive in the aquarium. A puma escaping the flames, only to be shot to death by a frightened housewife in Lützowplatz.

Ivanito settled with Pilar on a bench next to the tropical aviary. A pair of hyacinth macaws clambered along a perch, screeching back and forth.

"But why is she back now, do you think?"

"Who the hell knows? It's been twenty years. Maybe the loneliness was too much for her." The scrawnier macaw pecked at its mate. "What if the afterlife is just another Communist revolution to which she also doesn't belong?"

Pilar snorted. "Then we're all seriously fucked."

Even despondent, Ivanito laughed out loud. He thought about how his mother—a minimally talented, apolitical hairdresser—had been judged useless by the Revolution. Evaluated out of existence. Branded an "undesirable element" for wanting to live how she wanted without interference from the state. Where else might she have fled?

"Do you love her?"

The question took Ivanito by surprise. He recalled the time he'd gotten scarlet fever and stayed in bed for a week, delirious with dreams. Mami had cared for him, given him ice chips to soothe his throat, cool cloths for his sandpapery rashes. She'd fed him guarapo and coconut cookies, trusting that the sugar would alleviate his symptoms. How could Ivanito admit that he'd loved no one more? That he was afraid of losing her all over again?

"Even at her worst, she had chispe," he sighed.

Pilar unwrapped a Kinder Bueno bar and offered half to Ivanito. They ate in silence. Then she pulled another bar from her backpack and they shared that, too.

"So, why are you here?" Pilar finally asked.

There were a thousand reasons why he was in Berlin, but no single one felt complete. Ivanito tried to explain how the city had felt immediately familiar to him—slashed in two, a flashpoint for the Cold War, an epicenter of mythmaking and forgetting. Like Cuba, it was persistent with divisions. Didn't Pilar feel this, too?

"Auf geht's, Mom!" Azul came running back, panting and happy. His trousers were too short. He'd probably grown an inch since arriving in Berlin.

They smelled the polar bear enclosure before entering it. The bears were polishing off a rank lunch of herring and smelts. The place was jammed with visitors. The mystery of the missing Bertha and her keeper was stoking a frenzy of speculation: *It's a Communist trick, ohne Zweifel! Our mayor is to blame for this distraction! Die Stadt ist bankrott! Ach, haven't you heard? An American producer lured our Bertha to Hollywood!*

Ivanito stopped dead in his tracks. Straight ahead, lounging on the craggy rocks with a troika of polar bears, was his mother, lavishly wrapped in a white fur coat. Her towering bouffant was adorned with gardenias. She wore white vinyl go-go boots with steel spurs. As she lit a cigarette—Scheisse, she'd pinched his Marlene Dietrich holder!—phosphorescent smoke floated toward the clueless visitors.

"Don't play innocent with me!" Ivanito yelled, startling the on-lookers. What else had Mami stolen from him? He'd kill her if she took his flapper cocktail dress! "I'm done with your games!" Ivanito swiveled in desperation, looking like another Verrückte obsessed with the missing polar bear.

Murmurs rippled through the crowd. Was this madman address-ing them? A few cast furtive glances in his direction, but the bears weren't the least bestirred by Ivanito's outburst. His mother looked deeply offended, but nobody could see her but him. There was a menacing air about her, unspecific but threatening. A tall, wrought-iron fence and a moat of turbid water separated them.

"Is that Bertha?" Azul asked, awestruck.

Mami shifted her attention to the boy, who stared back reveren-tially. Her face softened but lost none of its shrewdness. She beheld Azul's beauty and innocence, his zest for adventure. Around them, nothing stirred—not a bear, not a breeze, not a single flaunting maple leaf. Silence descended, a velvety absence that Ivanito had only ever heard in music, as in the prologue to Monteverdi's *L'Orfeo*, when La Musica sings: *Non si mova augellin fra queste piante / Ne so'oda in queste rive onda sonante . . .*

His mother blew a slow-motion kiss to Azul. It was all the en-couragement Azul needed. In a flash he clambered over the fence like a capuchin monkey and rapturously jumped into the water. The polar bears registered the splash. Galvanized, perhaps, by the distant toll of instinct, they trundled to the water's edge on their gigantic, black-padded paws. The largest one slipped into the moat, its wedge-shaped head leisurely skimming the scummy surface. Its companions sat on their rumps to watch.

After a stunned hush, the spectators started screaming in six languages. Pilar kicked off her sneakers and catapulted over the fence, falling backward onto the concrete moat. Dazed, she rolled into the water with an unceremonious plop. Mein Gott! Was she drowning? A visiting church choir from Magdeburg launched into Bruckner's "Ave Maria" in a desperate attempt to distract the approaching bear.

Finally, Pilar emerged from the murky depths, spewing water, her left arm secured across Azul's chest. The onlookers burst into applause. Then she clumsily swam with her son toward the fenced side of the moat, a crushed pond lily in her hair. (A water nymph she was not!) Aaahhh-men, the choir sang as the trills of police whistles bore down on them from the east. If the bears hadn't been digesting their midday meal, who knew if events might not have taken a more tragic turn?

Ivanito stood rooted to the spot, a hand clamped to his mouth. His halo crackled with electricity, overheating his scalp. A copper crash of cymbals reverberated in his brain. Mami was to blame for this. Crash. Nobody else. Crash, crash. His ruin was at hand. Crash, crash, crash, crash.

⁓

Hours after Pilar and Azul went to bed, a puffy-eyed Ivanito was chain-smoking Camels and staring out his bedroom window, woeful and ashamed. He'd fled the polar bear enclosure before the police arrived, fearing that they would drag him to a nuthouse if he tried to explain what'd happened. Then Ivanito hid inside a Kurfürstendamm cinema, which was playing, impossibly, the new Almodóvar film, *All About My Mother*. He watched it twice with a clenched jaw. His behavior—cowardly in the extreme—was unforgivable.

Later, Ivanito learned that die Politzisten had pointlessly shot tranquilizer darts at the polar bears and cordoned off the enclosure with crime-scene tape. That they'd interrogated a shivering Pilar and Azul, wrapped in foil thermal blankets, along with the Magdeburg choir. That a brief cloudburst had disrupted the proceedings. That the local press stampeded to the zoo, then luridly featured the incident in the tabloids and on the evening news. That his cousins, fortunately, were spared arrest.

Ivanito couldn't stop apologizing to Pilar, who remained withdrawn all evening. This unnerved him more than any outright wrath. (In her punk days she'd been known to smash a chair or two.) He picked up borscht and dark-rye bread for dinner—his Russian comfort food—and an Erdbeerkuchen for dessert, of which Azul had four slices topped with Schlagsahne. Pilar was unimpressed. Then Ivanito spent hours putting ice packs on her monstrous bruise, which extended from below her kidneys to her shoulder blades and looked painfully, hideously, tie-dyed.

Only Azul seemed unaffected by the day's excitement (the press had nicknamed him "Eisbärchen," which didn't displease him). He was running a low-grade fever but seemed content enough to entertain himself in Ivanito's walk-in closet. Azul reveled in his uncle's hundred-plus hat collection: outrageous and demure, with feathers and without, seductively veiled, or piled high with kitschy accoutrements, including a glass rooster brooch.

There was no moon to speak of. It was quiet outside except for a man in a sheepskin shapka running barefoot down Kaiserdamm. Once, Ivanito had lost a boot jumping onto a tram in Moscow. It was November, and already well below freezing. By the time he hobbled back to his rented room and soaked his foot in warm water, the frostbite had nearly claimed his toes. Then, as now, he played

Prokofiev's *The Love for Three Oranges* to settle his nerves. Ivanito finished the pack of Camels and started another.

The chrome-and-glass grandfather clock struck five. His only solace at this hour was the sight of his books, which were arranged by language in sturdy wall-to-ceiling bookcases. There were hundreds of volumes, yet vastly fewer than what he'd actually read, forced as he'd been to abandon them in previous cities. Pushkin, Gogol, Tolstoy, Chekhov, Bulgakov . . . they were more precious to him than any lover, or friend.

Ivanito paced the bedroom as his halo alternately stuttered and pinged. Fussily, he rearranged the shirts in his Biedermeier dresser, though they were already neatly stacked. What stunt would his mother pull next? (She had all of eternity to plot against him!) Could he prevent her from committing some unspeakable act? Dismantle the destructive machinery of their past—its cogs and levers, its ejection points?

What was Mami offering him, anyway? An idealized death to make up for the life she'd botched on earth? The daily catastrophes of being her son? How tired he was of her convenient amnesias, of her claims to having protected him! She was the one who'd needed *his* protection! As a child he'd been her defender, her confidant, her private dance partner. Everything a boy shouldn't be. Yet for a time he'd also been the center of her world—and that had meant everything to him.

Ach, it was clear that he wasn't going to get any sleep tonight, even with the double dose of valerian. Ivanito considered sneaking off to the all-night karaoke bar in Kreuzberg, or over to that retro disco in Neukölln, with its baby-oiled men in silvery shorts dancing in cages. One drunken night, Ivanito had commandeered a cage, to considerable hooting and hollering. Or perhaps he should pay a visit to Saint Sebastian's, the basement dungeon in Friedrichshain with its cactus scapularies and Code Blue Room?

But how could he risk leaving Azul unguarded? Noch nie! He

must remain vigilant, sleep with one eye open, if necessary, to protect his nephew. No, he wouldn't let his mother get near Azulito.

Ivanito collected a pile of bedsheets from his linen closet and began shrouding the mirrors in his apartment, hoping to ward off another ghostly visit. Flickering in the mirrored mahogany armoire was an elegant couple dancing a bolero son. How languidly they drifted over the checkered tile floor, dreamy-eyed and in love. Was he imagining the melody to "Lágrimas Negras"? The music swelled briefly, then stopped. The pair receded into the shadows. Reluctantly, he draped a black satin sheet over where they'd just been.

It was almost dawn when Azul stumbled into Ivanito's bedroom (was he sleepwalking?) and crawled under the eiderdown comforter, mumbling something in Turkish. The boy's steady breathing soothed him. It was as if his own younger self were rising inside him like a watchful shadow, observing them both. Ivanito sensed their histories converging, past and present melding into a dangerous, borderless whole.

Irina del Pino

Berlin

Irina waited impatiently for her sister by the Soviet War Memorial on the eastern edge of the Tiergarten. In her pocket was the photograph of Javier del Pino holding her as an infant. Would the image reassure Tereza, or devastate her? After two months apart, Irina worried sometimes that her twin might be a trick of the mind—a manifestation of longing, or lunacy. Everything she'd once accepted as rational was no longer true.

The morning after the tango dance, Irina had returned to Moscow to manage her lingerie factory. She and Tereza spoke on the phone nearly every day, comparing histories, arguing politics (her sister was a committed Socialist; Irina had zero class consciousness left), and planning this reunion. Meanwhile she'd bribed a Ministry of Health official to expedite the delivery of her birth certificate from Prague. It showed, unequivocally, that Maminka had given birth to just one child: *her*.

How had Tereza disappeared from official records?

The war memorial was ostentatious, designed to twist history to its lies. Irina mistrusted any official displays of heroism, or nationalism. She circled the requisite tanks and howitzers and inspected the dedication to the eighty thousand Soviet soldiers who'd died storming Berlin in 1945. What the plaque conveniently omitted was that

Stalin and Hitler had been allies during the first two years of the war, carving up Poland between them. So, the enemies of the dead built monuments to their victims? Pozhaluysta.

Before perestroika and glasnost, the Soviet Union had been defined, and unified, by war. But what defined Russia today? What did its people want? A greater selection of salamis? The frivolous option of tangerines? Mansions on the Black Sea, like those of the nation's oligarchs and kleptocrats? Irina was no fan of these crooks, but what use was idealizing the past? In her opinion, pragmatic capitalism—not the rampant thievery disguised as such—was Russia's best long-term solution.

The skies threatened rain and the wind was picking up, snapping notched leaves off the horse-chestnut trees. Irina pulled her hair into a loose topknot and fanned her neck, though the day was unseasonably cool. At last she spied Tereza in the distance, the Brandenburger Tor behind her, rushing over with a black umbrella tucked under her arm. The two embraced for a long time, as if making certain the other was real.

"Ready?" Tereza asked.

A short walk away, her mother was languishing in a nursing home in Mitte. It had been Tereza's idea to show up together and startle Mutti into telling them the truth. Was Elsa Meier the architect of their separation? The gatekeeper to their origin story? The twins turned onto Wilhemstrasse. A Turkish boy hawked a flat of strawberries in flawless German. Irina handed him a twenty-mark note and waved away the change.

The nursing home sat on the foundation of a prewar building pockmarked with bullet holes. Berlin's past was frequently visible beneath the obliterating new architecture, like geopolitical cross-sections. A pair of stag antlers was mounted on the wall behind the reception desk, macabre and menacing. More disturbing still was the mechanical parrot in a brass cage squawking: *Willkomen, alle zusammen!*

Asleep in her cramped top-floor room, Elsa Meier appeared shrunken to a fraction of her once-hulking self. It was difficult to imagine this old woman ever having had a scandalous affair, as Tereza reported, with a married taxidermist. (Apparently, he'd once gifted her a remarkably lifelike badger for her birthday.) On the nightstand was a small plaster bust of Lenin, a potted hyacinth, and a handful of green Soviet mechanical pencils. Geraniums drooped in the window boxes. Would these be the last living things Elsa Meier saw?

"Mutti, it's me. I brought someone here to see you."

Her mother's eyes fluttered open but appeared glazed, without recognition. She'd remained a single mother throughout Tereza's childhood and had deflected her neighbors' disapproving stares with despotic fastidiousness. This included washing her daughter's pet goldfish under the kitchen faucet every night.

Tereza dangled a strawberry under her mother's nose. Mutti sucked it into her mouth, stem and all, then proceeded to mash it with her gums. The juice trickled down her faded housedress. Tereza fed her more strawberries until a nurse stuck her head in the door and warned of diarrhea.

"Bitte, hör mir zu," Tereza scolded, but Mutti was fixated on the strawberries. "That's enough for now. The nurse says too many will make you sick."

Irina felt a glassy hammering in her brain, as if long-suppressed memories were pushing their way to the surface. Blyad'! Had she met Elsa Meier before? Was she the thief who'd stolen her baby sister from the hospital? And why had she picked (or illegally gotten) Tereza, and not her? Irina shuddered to think of the alternate life she'd narrowly missed.

"Stand next to me," Tereza whispered. "Let her see us together."

The twins lined up shoulder to shoulder, giving Mutti time to register their presence. She grew stock-still. Only her rheumy, unblinking eyes darted between the two.

"Tell us what you know." Tereza's tone was cautious. "We stand before you, proof of what you've hidden."

Her mother's face shut down, stared back with a stubborn silence. What other weapon did she have? Irina would've gladly shaken the crone upside down until the truth clattered out of her like loose coins. Mutti rubbed her eyes, lay back on her pillow, and stared at the ceiling with a disagreeable expression. This was going nowhere.

Then without warning she began singing in a reedy voice: *Auferstanden aus Ruinen / und der Zukunft zugewandt, / laß uns dir zum Guten dienen . . .* Tereza turned to Irina, mouthing: "East German national anthem." It was like sitting in the empty ruins of a theater watching the last performance on earth.

"For peace and socialism—be prepared!" Mutti snapped.

"Always prepared!" Tereza responded reflexively.

Her mother raised a feeble fist. "Solidarity with the international working class!"

"Das reicht, Mutti."

Irina held her tongue. If she wasn't careful, more would come out of her mouth than was prudent. She and her sister were living on hourglass time, she reminded herself, each grain precious after everything they'd lost. Obviously, Tereza had taken socialism's promises to heart. If she needed to do a song and dance about the GDR, so be it.

"I had a dream," the old woman said, absently inspecting her slack belly.

"What was it, Mutti? What did you dream?"

The mother gaped at Irina. "That there were two of you, Liebling. Two beautiful girls just for me."

Irina's head was spinning. The fucking sow! Was she taunting them with a pseudo-confession? Manipulating a fake "dream" of her crime? How Irina itched to knock that blunt bulb of a nose off her face!

But Tereza's eyes begged her to say nothing.

"Tell me more about the dream."

Her mother sank back against the pillows, patient as ancient stone.

"I'm an expert in polyethylene, you know," Mutti proclaimed, apropos of nothing. She'd been a chemist in an East Berlin Kombinat for twenty-six years before a stroke and the ensuing memory loss—worsened by the shock of the Mauerfall—grew severe enough to warrant assisted living.

"Ja, ich weiß das." Tereza pulled the blanket over her mother's knees, leaving her bare feet exposed. Ugh. There was something grossly indecent about Elsa Meier's gouty toes. Tereza fidgeted with the broken zipper on her backpack and unwrapped a Mettwurst brötchen. Mutti's eye's lit up. She wolfed it down so fast she nearly choked.

"It's time for you to rest now."

"Naja, sleep, sleep," Mutti muttered, a bit of the spreadable sausage clinging to her chin. "I might as well be dead." Then she closed her eyes, hummed a snatch of a lullaby ("Der Mond Ist Aufgegangen"), and pretended to sleep.

◦──◦

The café had an elegant 1920s Viennese ambience, as if the destructions of World War II had never happened. Lively waltzes played in the background, interspersed with Wienerlieder and an occasional polonaise. Irina ordered more coffee. It was rich and strong, better than anything in Moscow.

"I couldn't get out of there fast enough," she admitted. "I know she raised you but—"

"But what?"

Irina pulled back. After all, her sister wasn't to blame here. She refused to let Tereza's mother sabotage their relationship. Her own mother hadn't exactly been any sort of model, either. Maminka returned from Kabul addicted to the morphine she'd administered to dying Soviet soldiers. Gone was the woman who'd read Chekhov, hunted portobellos big as dinner plates, treated Irina to Friday-night pedicures with towels and buckets of warm, sudsy water in their communal kitchen.

"It's just that . . . it could very well have been me in your place."

"Neither of us had our rightful lives," Tereza said.

Irina thought back—as she had a thousand times—to the tango party, to the impossible odds of their meeting. Was it a mistake to dredge up the wreckage of their pasts? Could they adjust to the gaps they might never know?

"It frustrates me that I can't document what happened," Tereza said. "But what can I do if Mutti doesn't remember?"

"Or is determined to forget." Irina slid the photo of Javier del Pino across the table.

Her sister stared hard at it, as if she could bring it to life. There was no denying their resemblance, down to the telltale moles on their cheeks.

"Unglaublich." Tereza was barely audible in the din of the café. "Even my learning tango was fueled by a false assumption."

Pedestrians waited out a violent downpour under Café Einstein's awning. The waiters raced by in their black-and-white uniforms, trays aloft with tempting Wiener schnitzels, marinated beef salads, Sacher tortes.

"I spent two months in Buenos Aires trying to find a father who didn't exist. Mutti let me go through that charade without a word of discouragement! So ein Mist!" Tereza wiped her eyes. "And yet I need to forgive her. You know, she was orphaned as a baby in the last months of the war. Her life wasn't easy."

"Spare me her victimhood—" Irina stopped herself.

"And she tried to give me everything. I was the first in my school with roller skates."

"She stole your identity."

"I love her. What choice do I have?"

"Falsified who you were. Silenced you."

"If I can't love her, then what do I have left?" Tereza looked stricken. "My country vanished overnight, Irina. And with it, my own history. I've lost my life twice."

Irina's cell phone rang—it was her new factory director in Moscow. Masha Nikolayevna reported that nine employees had been stealing warehouse stock to sell on the black market. Irina decided to let Masha handle it. Wasn't that why she'd promoted her?

Irina ended the call and turned to her sister. "I thought archivists were supposed to be objective and sensible."

"Ja, but only with archives."

"Well, there's nothing sensible about your tango!" she teased. Tereza was a different person when she danced—free, sexy, confident.

"Poor Mutti is already a ghost."

"That's what she'd like you to believe. It would let her off the hook."

"What if this lie was the one irregular act of her life?"

"An act that lasted twenty-nine years? It wasn't just one thing but a million things!"

"What about *your* mother?" Tereza lashed out. "What was her role in all this?"

Irina was rattled by the accusation. Maminka was imperfect but she would've never surrendered her own child. "I can't imagine her giving you up."

"There are lots of things we can't imagine—and yet they happened. Didn't she steal you away from your father?"

"*Our* father."

"We have to reconsider everything we thought we knew. The facts—even if we could establish them—never tell the whole story."

Irina called over their waiter and ordered the Leberkäse with potato salad. Her sister asked for a club sandwich with pommes frites. They were similar in this, too: their appetites spiked under stress.

"A part of me always knew you existed." Tereza's voice dropped to a whisper. "As a child, I used to draw double self-portraits, one after another. As if there were always two of me. The drawings would upset Mutti but she never told me why. When I met you, everything finally made sense to me. I made sense to me. It was you I'd been missing all along."

Irina had never intuited a missing "other." Was this a deficiency on her part? Or had her father's absence crowded out every other loss?

"Do you think he knew there were two of us?" Tereza asked.

Irina scrutinized the picture of their father again. "Could he have looked so happy if he'd known one of us was missing from the picture?"

They ate in silence, the photo between them. Without asking permission, they plucked food off each other's plates: a strip of bacon here, a dollop of Kartoffelsalat there.

"I have news." Tereza leaned in, her mood lifting. "A discovery from this morning. It's why I was late."

"Tell me."

"I was researching the Cuban side of our family when I came across this."

Irina scanned the blurry printout. "Who is it?"

"We have a cousin in Berlin."

"What?"

"Our father's nephew, the son of his sister Felicia."

"I can't believe it! Eto bizumiye!"

"He's a performer."

"A singer?"

"A drag queen. He's also a translator. Four languages, including Russian."

"Russian?" Irina was incredulous. "How did you find this?"

"Sometimes, Liebe, it's easier to track down the living than the dead."

3

Pilar Puente

Berlin

It was a miracle we stayed in Berlin after that stunt Ivanito pulled at the zoo. What a weasel! He took off just as the cops were storming over with their whistles and dart guns. Luckily, Azul got us out of that circus with his playground German. In total shock—and with my back psychedelically bruised—I packed our bags, dead set on catching the next flight to L.A. But Ivanito wouldn't hear of it. He launched a nonstop self-mortification campaign, forswearing cigarettes (temporarily, it turned out) and threatening to lash himself with a whip.

It worked. Because here we were, two weeks later—still together, still family.

Ivanito's next drag show was opening in June and he was frenetically rehearsing around the clock. Azul had become his shadow, his pint-size adjutant—lip-synching along to La Lupe's songs, running the choreography, choosing costume trimmings. With pudgy hands clutched to his heart, feigning forsaken love, Azul was alarmingly convincing. It went beyond mimicry and tactical palm fronds. He was really feeling those lyrics!

Sé que guardaste tu carcajada más brutal
Para anunciarle al mundo entero mi final . .

And what was I—the resident Hausfrau—doing amid this melo-drama? Repairing a Meissen porcelain platter from the 1930s, which Azul accidentally knocked over during a vigorous rumba. What other mother of a six-year-old had to deal with this? Azul slashed his knee falling on the porcelain shards, too. The resulting scar was identical to the one on Ivanito's knee, which pleased them both. Like matching jumbo shrimp, they agreed.

The platter was hand-painted with vermilion dragons in the chi-noiserie style once popular in Europe. On its reverse side, crossed blue swords attested to its authenticity. All pedigree aside, it felt good to mend what was broken, to hold an object in my hands that I could transform. It made me want to shape a lump of clay again, or guide a saw blade through stone. To get back to my studio, back to work.

I'd heard about kintsugi as an undergrad. It was an ancient Japa-nese technique of restoring broken pottery with seams of amalgam-ated gold. I fantasized about traveling to Kyoto, apprenticing with the masters. Could I push kintsugi in new sculptural directions? Breathe life into a venerable tradition? Reassemble my piles of shards into improbable, abstract objects? I knew how arrogant I sounded, but nothing had excited me this much in years. *Only work which is the product of inner compulsion can have spiritual meaning.*

Thank you, Walter Gropius.

Ivanito and Azul were shimmying to another La Lupe number, a lively guaracha. I regretted never learning how to dance—yet another marker of being a fake Cuban. Ivanito had picked up his moves from his mother, Tía Felicia, swaying and swooning his childhood away to Beny Moré's boleros. Now he could dance to anything, and with anyone. Ages ago, I'd watched him perform a flawless mambo with my mother, who was also—I hated to admit—a fantastic dancer.

My own specialty was jumping in place like a pogo stick while si-multaneously pumping my fist in the air. In the epic mosh pit of our band Autopsy's inaugural show at the Mudd Club, I dove from the stage into the crowd. Damn, if I didn't crack a rib, but it was the craziest party! How Ivanito escaped injury that night remained a mystery.

"Did you know," he said without missing a dance step, "that the Soviets' electronic radar station in Cuba was called LOURDES SIGNIT? For 'Signals Intelligence.'"

"What the fuck?"

"The ironies never cease."

The landlady banged a broom on the ceiling from her apartment below. Ivanito called her the Mandrill on account of her chronically inflamed nostrils. That she-monkey complained about everything: her utilities bills; our noise level; the garlic stink in the stairwell. Ivanito paid her a monthly supplement for the extra heat and water he used for his plants. I threw in another twenty marks a week to offset the rest. Thankfully, the Mandrill was heading off soon to visit her sister in Tübingen.

Most days Ivanito, Azul, and I wandered around the city—to the Gendarmenmarkt, or the Tiergarten, or the Spree amusement park. Its shuddering roller coaster was a relic from GDR days and the Ferris wheel had fifty-mile views of Berlin, from the high-rises of Neukölln to the Reichstag's sparkling ultramodern dome. On Sundays we went to sing karaoke at Mauerpark, or attended the weekly Her Queer Majesty Tea in Friedrichshain, where Ivanito was treated like royalty.

The contemporary art scene was flourishing but nothing wowed me. I was far more intrigued by the raw art on the Wall's East Side Gallery, like that mural of Brezhnev and Honecker locked in a kiss and titled *My God, Help Me to Survive This Deadly Love*. Ivanito and I admired a lot of the same living artists—Nan Goldin, Annette Messager, Louise Bourgeois, for starters—and we were passionately aligned against the despicable Jeff Koons.

But it was a special exhibit on Weimar artists that astounded me: Hannah Höch's subversive photomontages (*From Above* and *Flight*);

the disturbing images of Christian Schad (*Self-Portrait*) and Otto Dix (*Metropolis* and *To Beauty*). And I was impressed by how Max Beckmann (*Paris Society*) and George Grosz (*Eclipse of the Sun*) distilled the era's madness and desolation into singular visions. All of them embodied what Haru once told me were the two elements of great art: revulsion and reverence.

I understood this better now than when he'd said it.

Ivanito's grandfather clock struck midnight. Time was up—but for what, exactly? It was past Azul's bedtime but impossible to get his attention. He and Ivanito were in the middle of another high-octane rumba. Who was I to break up their fun? And how the hell had I become that person who shut down the party?

"Time to go to sleep," I said miserably.

"Just one more dance, Mom!" Azul pleaded, then slapped his butt like La Lupe.

Ivanito bribed ten more minutes out of me with a bottle of brandy labeled PEOPLE'S OWN DISTILLERY. It tasted as bad as it sounded. Barely mollified, I returned to the broken platter. The epoxy I was using to piece it back together deadened the hand-painted dragons, so I mixed it up with a little rainbow glitter from my cousin's vanity. What I really wanted to do was shatter the platter again and create something altogether different.

Just before bedtime, Ivanito decided I needed a curtsy lesson. "Because," he declared, "you don't make enough of an impression coming or going."

Right. Like this was my ultimate goal in life.

"Now, stand up, Pilar. Enough with your slouching already! Hold out your arms like a prima ballerina."

I groaned.

"Do it, Mom!" At this rate, Azul would grow up to be a drag queen, too, or else a five-star general.

I strained for a modicum of grace but my knees cracked as I awkwardly bent forward.

"They could hear that in the balcony!" Azul clicked his tongue
like his uncle. Thank you, oh precious flesh of mine.

"The back of the balcony," Ivanito corrected. Then he demon-
strated the lushest, most floating-on-air curtsy I'd ever seen. How
did he do that—and in stiletto mules?

Azul fell asleep trussed up in his ostrich-feather boa. What
need did he have of stuffed animals anymore? Or bedtime stories? I
watched him sleeping and hoped he'd be okay. I loved him, fiercely.
But was I too permissive? Did he need a father, like Mom insisted?
I told myself that Azul was having the time of his life in Berlin,
obsessed with Cuban divas and polar bears and learning German.
Things could be a lot worse.

I removed my glue-speckled apron and beckoned Ivanito to sit
with me on the burgundy sofa. To my surprise, he rested his head
on my shoulder. Neither of us spoke for a while. It was an age-old
tradition for Cuban mothers to fasten onyx pins on their babies'
diapers against the evil eye. Mom and Tía Felicia had complied,
but perhaps what we'd needed more were mal de ojos against *them*.

"Do you ever think about that moment?" I asked.

"You mean the Peruvian embassy?"

Ivanito knew exactly what I meant.

"I've always wondered if I did the right thing."

It was the great divide of his life. Ivanito was barely thirteen and
his mother had just died. He was confused, despondent, vulnerable.
Mom took advantage of that vulnerability to steal him away in the
middle of the night, right under Abuela Celia's nose. Early the next
morning my grandmother and I raced over to the embassy, determined to bring him home. What we found were thousands of defec-
tors jam-packed on the embassy grounds, all hoping for a chance to
get out of Cuba.

It was a miracle I found my cousin at all.

Ivanito lifted his head off my shoulder and looked at me for a long time, as if reliving the moment. "I was terrified to go," he said, finally, "but I was more terrified to stay."

"Your heart was beating so fast when I hugged you."

"When I saw you, I knew I had to go."

"But what if you'd stayed?"

The oven timer went off. Ivanito was reheating a broiled squab.

"Mami was dead. What was left for me in Cuba?"

"I lied to Abuela, told her I hadn't seen you. Of course, she knew the truth."

His first life ended that day, and the second one began. I felt guilty for helping him escape the island. It permanently estranged me from Abuela Celia. Would I have done it again, given the opportunity? In retrospect, the episode felt so tainted by and entangled with my mother's agenda that it was hard to know for sure. But yes, I probably would.

Ivanito's journey to New York took two grueling months. No time to say good-bye to anyone, or anything. A brutal uprooting. By chance he'd grabbed his mother's blank diary. Tucked inside was a photo of her looking young and beautiful on the beach at Santa Teresa del Mar. It was the only photo of her he still had. Nothing else to show where he'd come from, no evidence of everything he'd lost. After his first desolate months in Brooklyn, Ivanito was convinced that he was un-transplantable.

"You were a mess," I said.

"You took me under your wing."

I held Ivanito close, like when he was thirteen and lonely and homesick in New York (as if being thirteen weren't hard enough). Ultimately, it was our solidarity against my mother that bonded us.

"Lourdes Puente had big plans for you," I deadpanned. "*Imagínate, mijito, you could manage my Yankee Doodle bakeries from coast to coast!*"

My impersonation was spot-on. That, at least, made him laugh.

I reminded Ivanito how irresistible he became in New York a short time later, an exotic Cuban "other." In those days, "Where are you from?" was an ordinary question, not the provocation it later became. Even during the ravages of the AIDS years, Ivanito behaved as if he had extra lives to spare. All the while he never stopped thinking about his shadow life, the one he'd left behind in Cuba.

I climbed into bed but I was too exhausted to sleep. I thought about Haru and how he'd left me barricaded against romance. This kind of obsessive, ruinous love ran in my family. Abuela Celia had her Spaniard. Ivanito had his Russian dancer. And I was stuck with the vanished Haru. Our pasts littered with heartbreak's debris. Were our fates a family curse? Or were we lucky to have known passion at all?

Haru told me once about yūrei, ghosts who were trapped between this world and the next, in a purgatory of unfinished business. It might've applied to us except for the fact that we remained marooned on Planet Earth.

Azul twitched beside me, his lips silently moving, a miniature replica of his father. I longed to dream what he dreamt, fly with him to wherever he flew. But there were things I would never know about him. And these unknown things would multiply with each passing day, each passing year, until we became loving, receding strangers to each other—a mother-and-son mystery.

4

Irina del Pino

Berlin

It was Irina's idea to go out to the lesbian club that night. The ordeal with Tereza's mother had left her more exhausted than a month of work at her Moscow factory did. Now it was time to relax, to let loose, to find pleasure in life again. Her sister wasn't easy to convince, but Irina hadn't ascended to lingerie royalty by settling for refusals. To her, a "no" was an invitation, a challenge, the opening move in a dance of seduction. Plus she'd worn a black corset under her jumpsuit for extra luck.

The club was near Winterfeldtplatz. Tereza claimed that its name—Alles Ist Möglich—came from a famous graffiti slogan painted on a dilapidated wall in Mitte. Irina certainly tried to live as if everything were possible. It was her de facto motto. Stepping inside the club felt like descending into a fluorescent, weightless realm. A tempting array of girls—lipsticks, butches, femmes, baby dykes—crowded the bar, which was presided over by a pale, flirty boi with bleached dreads.

"Give us your most original drink," Irina ordered.

"Are you sure you trust me? You might need a safe word."

"I have no use for safe words, Hübsche."

The bartender's cheeks mottled pink but she got to work, serving up two cocktails that tasted like a fusion of mint and kerosene.

"What do you call this?" Irina asked.

"No name yet. I just made it up."

"I think maybe I'll have a chardonnay." Tereza handed her cocktail to Irina, who downed it in one swallow. The ambient techno music alternated, bizarrely, with Pink Martini, U2, and seventies punk. Half the club was drinking or dancing, the other half cruising like neon tetras. A buff woman in a ribbed tank top slapped a conga in the corner.

Irina turned to her sister. "What's the truth worth to you?"

"Clearly not as much as it is to you."

"But you're an archivist."

"Not of Mutti's secrets—I told you already." Tereza barely touched her wine, as if she'd resolved to guard her sobriety. "She must have her reasons."

"What about the need for us to know what the fuck happened?"

"I don't need her remorse. And I refuse to torment her."

"Oh, please."

"She's on her deathbed. Can't you see that?"

"Then it's our last chance!" Irina hadn't wanted to start another argument but how could she give up now? "You're condemning us to ignorance, to darkness—"

"Which is what most of history is," Tereza interrupted. "It's delusional to think we can nail down the past. In any case, it's more about forgetting than remembering."

"Only *your* forgetting is willful!"

"Every archivist needs to discard what she deems useless."

"Useless? Blin!"

Her sister teared up. "We can't just squeeze the truth out of Mutti."

"Why don't you let me try?"

"Because you'd stop at nothing!"

Irina backed off. Her sister was right—that much she had to admit. She'd easily strangle that hateful witch to learn what she knew. A dandy in a bow tie and pencil mustache—very Weimar—invited Tereza to dance. It was jarring to watch her sister break loose to U2. Irina had never seen her dance to anything but tango.

> It's all right, it's all right, it's all right
> She moves in mysterious ways . . .

She dispatched her third mint-and-kerosene cocktail, then held up a finger for a fourth. How paradoxical was it that her archivist sister was willing to surrender their pasts while Irina, who'd survived by always keeping her eye on the future, insisted on reckoning with it?

A high femme in a fuchsia miniskirt occupied Tereza's empty barstool. The woman was petite, plush and velvety as a ring box. Before she could raise an eyebrow, Irina leaned over and whispered in her ear. "You're gorgeous. If you're still here in an hour, I'll come looking for you. I promise to make it worth your while." The proposition seemed to intrigue the woman, who smiled with charmingly crooked teeth before slipping back into the crowd.

Tereza returned to the bar, overheated by her dance with the exuberant fop. Fanning her face with a cocktail napkin, she picked up where they'd left off. "What if we don't have room for the truth?"

"Which you get to determine?"

"But what if we learn something . . . unforgivable?"

"It can't be worse than what I'm already imagining."

"I'm afraid," Tereza said bluntly.

"Fear is what's useless," Irina shot back. It made a person weak, she wanted to add, but refrained. Her mother had learned to fend off rapists (Russian soldiers, mostly) in Kabul with a loaded Tokarev, or get herself a "boyfriend" whether she wanted one or not. The stress had taken its toll, numbing her to the daily violence. Before she died, Maminka admitted: *I went halfway around the world to become a stone.*

"I'm afraid," Tereza repeated, more softly this time, "because the person in question, the person this would harm the most—and probably kill—is Mutti."

A tide of regret overwhelmed Irina. Why hadn't she fought for her own mother's life the way Tereza was fighting for hers? Might she have saved Maminka? Irina only knew that she couldn't let Elsa Meier die before she told them the truth.

"So, you're willing to forfeit our pasts to preserve her lies?"

"We found each other. Isn't that enough?" Tereza looked off at the frenetic dance floor, then back at her sister. "Bitte, don't judge me."

"You're the one judging me!"

"Irina, we just met two months ago."

"Nyet, dorogaya sestra. We met thirty years ago in our mother's womb. And we're inseparably bound, no matter why we were forced apart."

"I get that, but—"

"Remember your drawings, Tereza!" Irina held her sister's face—a perfect image of her own—and kissed her on both cheeks. "All we need is an answer to a simple question."

5

Azul Puente-Tanaka

Berlin

Who was that nuzzling his ear, breathing on his cheek? Azul opened his eyes and stared at the cow looming over his bed. It jolted him like a firecracker. Its muzzle was soft and warm and it yawned so wide its back molars were visible. The cow waggled its head, then slowly turned into that lady at the zoo. She still had gardenias in her hair, but instead of a fur coat, she wore a purple velvet cape.

"I'm your tía Felicia," she said. "Don't be afraid, mi cielo. You're safe with me."

But Azul wasn't afraid. His chest didn't hurt like it had when he'd really been afraid, like the time those fourth graders had beaten him up in the schoolyard. They'd held him facedown, punched his back, called him a sissy. None of the other kids defended him, or told the teachers.

"Where would you like to go?" Tía Felicia asked. "We can go anywhere, do anything."

Nobody had ever asked him that before. In school it was always *Sit here, Do that, Color inside the lines.* Stupid things. Here in Berlin he could do almost anything he wanted, especially with his uncle. How could he choose just one thing out of a million cool things to do?

"Are you a cow?"

"No, corazón. Whatever gave you that idea?"

He could see through Tía Felicia's face to the painting of a Prussian battle on the wall. Azul knew that she was Tío's mother. He complained all the time about the halo she'd stuck on his head. But did it have any secret powers? Could he get one, too?

"Where are you when you're not here?" Azul asked instead.

"Such a smart question, precioso. I guess you could say that I'm always here—and always not here." Her voice was as velvety as her cape.

"At the same time?"

"Exactamente."

"That doesn't make any sense!"

"Do you like to dance, my darling boy?"

Tía Felicia had changed the subject. Grown-ups did that all the time.

Azul didn't feel like dancing. He was tired from rehearsing with his uncle. But when Tía Felicia held out her hand, he took it. A ticklish feeling spread through his fingertips like static electricity. Before he knew it, they were floating into the living room. The windows flew open and Azul heard cats hissing in the street below. He and Tía Felicia drifted outside, climbing higher and higher into the skies until the moon and the stars seemed close.

"Ready to dance now?"

Azul giggled as his aunt twirled him around, then upside down. A meteor shower sparkled in the distance.

"You're my little Moon Rabbit," she said, coaxing him into another somersault.

This was way better than all the rides at Magic Mountain! Was his aunt a sorceress? Had she cast a magic spell on him?

"Wow! This is fun!" Azul's voice rippled into the night. He couldn't wait to tell Ozan and Lukas at the playground. Would they believe him, or call him ein Lügner?

"Do you want to see the polar bears?"

"At the zoo?"

"Where they live, in the wild."

"The North Pole?" Azul couldn't believe it.

"Ven, mi amor."

His aunt offered him two coconut cookies for the journey. "To keep up your strength," she said. They were delicious but made him thirsty, so Tía Felicia conjured up a glass of milk for him, too. When Azul finished, she held him by the waist and they traveled so fast that everything around them looked blurry. A loud screeching hurt his ears, but the trip didn't take long. Soon they were gliding over glaciers, their bodies casting long shadows on the ice.

Azul was enchanted.

"It's almost summer here," Tía said. "The sun shines all the time."

"There's no night?"

"Only an hour or two."

It was strange to be near this much ice but not feel the cold. In fact, Azul was getting kind of hot. He unbuttoned his pajama top halfway and felt the Arctic breeze on his chest. When he looked down again, three polar bears—like the ones at the zoo—were crouched by a hole in the ice. One of them looked up at him and raised its paw, as if to say hi.

Just then a ringed seal emerged from the water, and in an instant the biggest bear attacked it and dragged it onto the ice. Azul watched as the bears feasted on the dead seal. He was sad for the seal but happy for the bears. Whose side was he on? He didn't like feeling so confused.

"I have one more place to show you." Tía Felicia squeezed his hand tight and kissed his forehead. The heat from her lips spread down his face.

Azul braced himself for another stormy flight, but the next part of the trip was smooth. He was losing track of time with all this flying around. Was it morning yet? Azul spied an albatross going south, like them, its wings outspread like an airplane's. There were thousands of other birds flying, too—ducks and geese and peregrines—in the opposite direction. He and his aunt flew through the flocks without crashing into them. Did this mean they were invisible?

"The birds return home every spring," Tía Felicia shouted over the honking.

"I don't ever want to go home!" Azul shouted back, but he wasn't sure where he meant anymore. Los Angeles felt so far away.

"Then we can wander the stars forever!"

Gradually, the ocean turned from a grayish blue to a bright turquoise, like those ice pops Mom refused to buy him. They coasted over an island covered with mountains and palm trees. "Those are the Guaniguanico Mountains," Tía said. "The best tobacco in the world grows here." Then she and Azul circled over a broken-down barn that smelled like poop and cigars. They flew inside and sat in the rafters with a small colony of bats. There were cows mooing in the stalls and an owl alert on its perch.

Below them a boy was lying on the floor, his face smashed against the hay, the backs of his legs smeared with blood. His red shorts were pulled down around his ankles. Three bigger kids were taking turns hurting him. They were mean like those bullies at school—kicking the boy, laughing and calling him names in Spanish. Tía Felicia watched intently, eating a wheel of pineapple. Her face was wet with tears.

"I would never let this happen to you, mi cielo." She offered Azul a bite of pineapple but his stomach hurt too much to eat.

"Who's that down there?" he asked, tapping his left ear.

"If only I'd known . . ."

"Make them stop!" Azul cried.

A trickle of pineapple juice dripped down Tía's jaw and onto the collar of her cape. "This happened a long time ago."

"Take me away from here! I want my mom!"

His aunt squinted at him. Did she think he was a crybaby? Would he have to escape by himself? But Tía Felicia hoisted him over her shoulders, piggyback-style. It felt bumpy under her cape, like crocodile skin, but he didn't dare complain. Azul put his arms around her neck, hard as the guardrail at school. They shot high into the skies, then sped all the way back to Tío's apartment in Berlin.

The windows were open, and they flew inside as if nothing unusual had happened. The minute hand of the grandfather clock jerked forward. Azul hopped off his aunt's back and was hurrying off to bed when she stopped him.

"There's coconut ice cream in the freezer. Don't you want some?"

Azul shook his head, not looking her in the eye.

"Don't let anyone tell you this didn't happen."

"I won't, Tía." He was eager to get away from her.

"I'm going to leave something behind as proof."

Azul watched a gigantic puzzle appear overhead, a replica of what they'd seen at the North Pole. With a sweep of her hand, she scattered the pieces all over the floor.

"When you finish the puzzle they'll know that what you've seen is true." Tía sounded strict and her face looked scary. "¿Me entiendes?"

Azul nodded. He was afraid of her now. "Okay, bye."

"Adiós, precioso." Then Tía Felicia spun in place until she was nothing but a feather of smoke and disappeared out the window, leaving behind an old-lady floral smell.

Azul stood still, blinking, then limped off to bed. His throat was sore and his knee was hurting again. He picked off what was left of his scab and curled up next to his mother, who was snoring loudly. "Hey, Mom, I'm back," he croaked in her ear. She mumbled his name and draped an arm over his shoulder.

GRANADA

Celia del Pino

In which the lovers check into a luxury hotel next to the Alhambra . . .

"It's a convent?" Celia asked. "Por dios, ¡qué religioso te has puesto!"

The hotel was on the grounds of the Alhambra, one of a chain of paradores—monasteries, castles, and historic buildings that had been adapted for tourists—sprouting up throughout Spain. White-washed archways connected the tiled Moorish courtyards with aviaries of chattering macaws and African parrots. A cavernous bar pulsed with music and a revolving mirrored ball. All this splendor made Celia nervous. She was unaccustomed to anything exceeding her expectations.

"First, you rest," Gustavo said. "Then I have a surprise for you."

"Another one?"

"I'm full of surprises, mi amor." Gustavo brought Celia's hand to his lips, as he often had at the Hotel Inglaterra, where he'd called her *mi reina, mi vida, mi corazón*. Below their window in the Parque Central, a trio from Santiago de Cuba had played bolero sons. At all hours the trio played and at all hours they had an audience, including that faithful campesina who returned daily to dance alone and wipe away her tears.

"How long will we be here?" Celia asked.

"Guess."

"Four days?"

Gustavo gave her what she took to be a smoldering look, though it might very well have been indigestion. Time will tell, Celia thought. They followed the bellhop to their room, the most magisterial in the hotel. A double balcony overlooked the Alhambra's palaces and gardens. The wrought-iron chandelier flaunted flame-shaped bulbs encased in oilcloth shades. On the dresser a nineteenth-century tellurion mechanically shifted its globe, moon, and stars. The bellhop set Celia's red suitcase on the banquette at the foot of the larger of two beds.

"I don't need all this space to sleep." Celia tried out the mattress, surprised at the coquettishness in her voice. Back in Santa Teresa del Mar she had only a narrow, sagging bed with sprung coils. "This bed is like a landing pad for a helicopter!"

Gustavo looked amused by her audacity. It seemed to Celia that he'd come with only the clothes on his back. Not until later would she discover that his necessities were already in place, that he'd managed every detail of their reunion—from the columnar candles, imposing as those in cathedrals, to the cante jondo playing softly in the background, to the sprigs of butterfly jasmine spilling from the ceramic pitchers. She patted the bed and looked at him invitingly.

"We have all the time in the world," Gustavo murmured, still standing.

"You said we have four days."

"Once, that was an infinite amount of time."

"Actually, it was quite finite." Celia stretched out on the bed and stared at the ceiling, reliving her disbelief as she'd watched her lover hurrying across the Parque Central, intent on abandoning her, on returning to Spain. Now the trio from Santiago, stationed below the balcony, was performing "Lágrimas Negras" with their guitars, their maracas, and their doleful voices. It became her anthem of sorrow.

How could Gustavo have left her without a word of explanation? He was married, of course. Celia knew that. And he'd felt

honor-bound to fight in his country's looming civil war. But why had
he been so damn *uncivil* about it? So heartless? That same spring
Celia took to her bed and stayed there for the next eight months,
determined to die.

"May I take off your shoes?" Gustavo knelt before her.

"Qué caballero," she said, her voice testy. "So, did you ever get
my first letter?"

Gustavo slipped off one of Celia's black patent-leather pumps,
then the other, and began massaging her feet. There was strength
in his hands, despite the arthritis.

"Ay, right there. That feels perfect." She blushed from the unin-
tended innuendo.

" 'November eleventh, 1934,' " he recited. " 'Mi querido Gustavo,
A fish swims in my lung. Without you, what is there to celebrate?
I am yours always, Celia.' "

"And all this time I imagined you never received it! That it had
gotten lost on the way, or that it was intercepted by—"

"By my wife?"

"Sí."

"Both, in fact, happened." He pressed her instep meaningfully.
"Your letter took months to arrive."

"Claro, like your first letter to me. From your purported deathbed, eh?"

"I was positively cadaverous, I swear!" Gustavo grinned with his
perfect, artificial teeth.

"And?"

"And Magdalena intercepted it. I never saw the letter until after
she'd died."

"But I wasn't dead."

"No. But I thought we had an understanding." He released
Celia's foot.

"An understanding without words? What kind of understanding
is that?"

Gustavo paused, as if wanting to carefully choose what he would say next. "Mi amor, the deepest understandings require no words."

Celia felt heat flushing through her surviving breast. The missing one was feeling prickly, too. Her phantom breast. Gustavo didn't know about it yet. One fraught revelation after another still to come. Por dios, why was she subjecting herself to such torments at her age? What if Gustavo had invited her here only to reject her all over again? Why wasn't she home, rocking on her wicker swing, guarding the north coast of Cuba?

"I wrote you many more letters," Celia said instead.

"What? I never received them!"

"Because I didn't send them. I kept them in a satin box under my bed. For twenty-five years I wrote to you, Gustavo, on the eleventh day of each month. Then I stopped."

Gustavo laid his head in Celia's lap. She found the fuzz on the nape of his neck curiously endearing, and caressed it. Their breathing evened, found a compatible rhythm.

"Don't you want to know why?" she asked.

"Because I left on the eleventh of April?"

"Yes, but I meant why I stopped writing?"

Slowly, Gustavo nodded. It stirred Celia, this leisurely movement of his head against her belly and thighs. How long had it been since she'd held anyone so close? Were those tears in his eyes, or hers? The last thing she wanted was for things to get maudlin.

"Soon after the Revolution triumphed, my first granddaughter was born. And I found my way. After so many lost years, I found my way."

"Do you still have those letters?"

"I gave them to Pilar."

Gustavo wrenched his neck to face Celia, his head pressing against her ribs. They looked like a classic portrait of the Madonna and Child except that the lights would need to be significantly dimmer to pull it off.

"I feel it."

"Feel what?" she asked.

"Your lost breast. It feels warmer than the remaining one."

Celia was taken aback. She tried to push him off her lap, but he clasped her hips.

"We're too old for modesty," he said.

The day's last light poured into the room, illuminating Gustavo's face. It looked serious, like a religious icon, with the expression of a martyr who'd chosen suffering over life.

"And you? What are you missing?" Celia bent over, straining her shoulder, and kissed him full on the mouth.

"I'm not missing anything. Not anymore."

Gustavo settled next to her on the bed. They kissed again, and again, eyes wide open. And for another hour, they kept on kissing— with bites and licks, their tongues playful, languorous. They kissed each other's eyes and foreheads, their earlobes and fragile jawlines. They didn't use their hands or remove a stitch of clothing, not even when dusk descended and shrouded them in a penumbral grace.

Celia came up for air first. "I know it's unromantic to say this but I'm thirsty as hell."

"Ha!" Gustavo barked like a seal. He retrieved a bottle of mineral water from the refrigerator and served it to her on a silver tray. "You're dehydrated, mi amor."

"Not everywhere," she teased.

Gustavo trailed a finger along her lips. "¿Tienes hambre?"

"Mucho."

"I'm in no rush. Are you?"

"I don't think waiting sixty-six years qualifies as rushing, Gustavo."

"Just a little longer."

"But we could drop dead any minute!"

"The Revolution has made you quite forthright, querida."

"This isn't about politics."

"Trust me?" Gustavo kissed the hollow of Celia's shoulder, inched his way up her neck to her ear, then pressed his ear to hers. "I can hear the ocean. Your ear is my shell."

"It's what I've listened to every day of my life."

"It's beautiful. So powerful."

"Sí, Gustavo. It is."

BERLIN

Ivanito Villaverde

Berlín

It was late morning when Ivanito woke up with a huge erection and a clanging halo. Both his dick and his head throbbed like hell. As he slipped out from under his comforter, the bedroom slowly flashed before his eyes like a deck of cards. This happened sometimes before a migraine. Ivanito pulled the black satin sheet off the mirrored mahogany armoire and admired his erection. If only he could go to the Tiergarten and work it off with emergency sex. But who knew what havoc his mother might wreak in his absence?

It was pouring outside and the wind was blowing the petals off a cherry tree. The living room curtains were wide open but it was too dim to see much. Ivanito felt something sharp-edged beneath his feet and switched on the lights. Verdammt! Hundreds of puzzle pieces were scattered everywhere. Most were white, like patchy snow, with a smattering of blacks and browns. Like abstracted polar bears, he thought. This had to be Mami's doing, but to what end? He anxiously scooped up the pieces, filling a trash bag.

Pilar stumbled past him into the kitchen to make coffee. Ivanito knew better than to utter a word to her until she'd had two cups, minimum. She was a perfect harridan before then. He could use a shot of rum but opted for a cigarette. Ivanito picked up the Meissen platter that Pilar had been repairing last night. What the fuck?

She'd pasted it together with his glitter glue! He stormed over to her, platter in hand. "I know you're probably working out something conceptually here but I want my platter back!"

"You're right." Pilar was suspiciously reasonable. "I *am* trying to work out something."

His cousin usually got defensive whenever Ivanito tried to talk to her about her work. Pilar had been stagnating for years, enraged by her failures, trapped by motherhood, forever stuck on that old Japanese artist—Azul's biological father—who'd abandoned her the minute he learned she was pregnant. It didn't help that Azul was a spitting image of him, down to his slightly jowly cheeks. Now Pilar was all enthused about kintsugi and talking about researching the pottery technique in Japan.

Bitte. Was this about Haru again?

"Hey, are you okay?" Ivanito asked, his anger dissipating. What did he care if Pilar spent her life fixing broken platters if it made her happy?

"I'm worried about Azul."

"That makes two of us."

"He wet the bed last night. That hasn't happened in years."

"Why do you think?"

"No offense, Ivanito, but I'm not sure I want him prancing around like a beauty queen. He's a little young—"

"Dress-up is for all ages, Liebchen."

"Ugh, don't call me that."

Ivanito couldn't believe where this conversation was going. Was Pilar really asking him to be less *gay* around her son? She, of all people? The one who'd gotten him to wear a dress in the first place? Who'd bought him his first jumbo carton of condoms? Just because her son had wet the bed? How was that his fault?

"Do you know who you sound like right now?" Ivanito was furious.

"Don't say it."

"You're on the brink of becoming your worst nightmare."

Ivanito grabbed the water mister and sullenly sprayed his peace lilies. He plucked dead leaves off the philodendron and ribbon dracaena, then put Mozart's Violin Concerto no. 3 on the turntable, hoping its euphony would invigorate his listless jungle and his own state of mind. He was immensely grateful to classical music, which he considered his fifth and most sacred language.

How had he withstood the clamor of punk for so long? Not to mention its moronic lyrics: *Sitting here in Queens / Eating refried beans . . .* Quatsch!

"I'm sorry," Pilar said quietly. "Why are you worried about Azul?"

Ivanito hesitated before answering. "I think my mother's after him."

"After him? How?"

Ivanito opened the trash bag and showed Pilar the deconstructed puzzle inside. She rummaged around, then picked up a piece, studying it like a riddle she had to solve.

"I don't get it."

"She was here. I found these on the floor when I woke up."

"They're not yours?"

"You think I have nothing better to do in the middle of the night?" Ivanito paced the perimeter of his hand-hooked Tetex rug, turning the corners like a Prussian soldier.

"Uh, they're all white."

"Sherlock Holmes you're not. I'm telling you, something happened here last night!"

"But how's Azul involved?"

"Mami's trying to lure him into following her." What more evidence did Pilar need? "You don't know what she's capable of!"

"A puzzle seems harmless enough."

"Nothing is harmless when it comes to my mother." Ivanito sniffed the air. "Don't you smell that? Gardenias. It's her signature scent."

"I do!" Azul ambled into the room. "It's that old lady's smell."

"What old lady?" Pilar asked.

"Tía Felicia."

Ivanito struggled to keep the fear out of his voice. "Did you see her last night?"

"Yep." Azul yawned, looking a bit pale. "What's for breakfast?"

"Whatever you want, conejito. So . . . she paid you a visit?"

"We went out."

"Out? Out where?" Pilar demanded.

"To the North Pole."

"What?"

"It was consensual, Mom."

Ivanito shot Pilar a confused look.

"She called me her Moon Rabbit."

Then they listened, speechless, as Azul described his transatlantic adventures. How he and Tía Felicia had watched a polar bear kill a seal, then eat it with his friends. How an albatross flew south, like them, to an island with mountains and palm trees. How they coasted into a barn and saw a boy getting hurt by three bigger boys. That was when Tía Felicia started crying, Azul said, and he begged to go home. She left him a puzzle to play with—"Where is it, anyway?"—as proof of what'd happened.

"Can I have scrambled eggs now?"

"Claro, conejito." The thought of their otherworldly globetrotting sickened Ivanito. And how had his mother flown twelve thousand miles in one night when just a few months ago she'd gotten hopelessly lost in Belarus?

Heat radiated from his halo, leached down his spine, branched through his nervous system. Sweat plastered his hair to the back of his neck. The halo was vibrating like a running motor, threatening to drive itself off his head. What he needed, immediately, was an ice-cold shower. Ivanito excused himself and stepped into the tub. He turned on the faucet, leaned against the tiles, let the water pour over his steaming halo, which sizzled as he cooled off.

Then he masturbated to calm down.

Fuck! The part about the boys in the barn? When had his mother known about that? Before her death? Or afterward, in a rush of omniscience? Wasn't it *because* of her that he'd been sent to boarding school in the first place? If she hadn't been declared an unfit mother, if she'd taken proper care of him, none of it would've happened. Mami hadn't noticed Ivanito's anguish when he returned home, either. She'd been too ill, too self-absorbed, too selfish to notice anything beyond her own troubles.

When he was feeling (increasingly) uncharitable toward his mother, Ivanito suspected her of varnishing their history with self-serving memories. Why, half the things she reminisced about hadn't even happened! Was this a subset of her narcissism? An attempt to give meaning to the fundamental emptiness of her role as a mother? Wasn't that how nostalgia worked? More critically, how could he stop her posthumous ataques de nervios? Release her grip on his life?

What his mother now seemed intent on was informing him that she knew every detail about him. That if he didn't submit to her, she would set her sights on Azul. The handwriting, Mami's handwriting, was on the wall: the boy was in play for her machinations. Ivanito was at the end of his rope. Al final de su cuerda. V kontse yego vervki. Am Ende seines Seil. He listened to the finale of Mozart's violin concerto, with its stirring resolution of oboes and horns.

While Pilar suspected that Azul's tale was nothing but a vivid dream, Ivanito knew better. Let them cart him off to the psychiatric ward at Charité Hospital! He believed his nephew's every word.

By midday the weather went from dreary to glorious. The rhododendrons were in full splendor. Ivanito was relieved to be outside, roving the aisles of the oldest flea market in Berlin, focused on anything but his mother. Der Strasse des 17 Juni Kunstmarkt sprawled over the western edge of the Tiergarten, a fifteen-minute walk from his place. Not the cheapest market, he told Pilar, because the vendors were savvy antiques dealers who knew the value of their inventory. But their offerings were decent, and they had piles of old porcelain: Meissen, Höchst, Wessel, Villeroy & Boch.

Pilar scoured the stalls overflowing with clocks, dishes, jewelry, cutlery, furniture, mirrors, all manner of bric-a-brac. There was even a kiosk selling chandeliers ripped out of Havana's mansions during these last hardship years of the Special Period. If Ivanito had money and a castle on the Rhine, he would fill it to bursting with collectibles, including as many vintage Decca records as he could find.

This flea market, Pilar remarked, didn't remotely resemble the ones in Los Angeles, where thirty years was considered prehistoric—for objects as well as people. Businesses proudly displayed signs saying ESTABLISHED IN 1982, as if that were an eternity ago.

Ivanito felt most at home in old cultures, surrounded by old things. In Russia and Germany, history was measured in centuries—and their crumbling courtyards reminded him of Old Havana. Growing up in postrevolutionary Cuba meant that his material world ranged from the eighteenth century (La Catedral de San Cristóbal; elaborate ironwork balconies) to the 1960s (Soviet-era apartment blocks that blunted all imagination). With its collapsing buildings and rubble everywhere, Havana looked decidedly postwar. Even the family house on Palmas Street, inherited from his great-grandparents, was more than a hundred years old, a leaking ruin painted a peeling canary-yellow.

It was midafternoon, late to be shopping. The best items would have been snapped up by early birds hours ago, morning rains notwithstanding. Ivanito's head ached and he bought a Spezi—a concoction of Coca-Cola and orange soda—at a Schnellimbiss to stave off another migraine. He pressed the cold bottle to his temple before taking a swallow. It soothed his hyperactive halo. Then he sat on a park bench and pulled out a paperback of *Dead Souls* to re-read. He needed the novel's comic relief, but found it impossible to concentrate.

Pilar kept inching along the stalls, picking up a dinner plate here, a soup tureen there—nothing extravagant, the more battered the better. It gave her a bargaining advantage with the dealers eager to get rid of their flawed stock. She paid a pittance for a brass table mirror with star-shaped crackles, as if it'd been pelted with pebbles. Ivanito was impressed by how indefatigably Pilar haggled (and in pidgin German), a skill no doubt inherited from her tightwad mother. How could the vendors imagine that this Amerikanische Turisten was buying their chipped, cracked wares only to break and then fix them?

Ivanito understood his cousin's need to repair broken objects, restore their integrity. Didn't he strive for that with every impersonation? Resurrect long-forgotten divas? Dust them off and reintroduce them to younger generations?

On summer solstice Ivanito would present another mid-century Cuban star: the wildly original La Lupe. A drag queen's dream, she was more gyration than gravitas, more irreverence than misery, the opposite of Olga Guillot's foreboding angel. La Lupe always performed to the point of near-collapse, and required oxygen after every show. Why bother taking the stage if you weren't willing to surrender your last breath? And La Lupe did, despite bankruptcy, paralysis, and late-in-life Evangelicalism.

From his bench Ivanito caught glimpses of Pilar and Azul as they wandered among the booths. Soon a minor drama erupted: Azul begged for a vintage toy troll from the ex-GDR, and Pilar, dangling the hideous thing from its oversize toes, refused him.

"It'll give you nightmares!" Pilar insisted.

"Worse than usual?"

Azul got the troll.

The trees were dazzling in their late-spring greens—poplars, lindens, birches, alders—all flourishing in the sandy Brandenburg soil. After the war, Berliners had chopped down the Tiergarten's forest for firewood during the bitterly cold winters of 1946 and 1947. Only a massive replanting effort in the fifties had saved it. Another Kriegsrückblicke surfaced before Ivanito's eyes: a brother and sister in patched-up coats were trying, futilely, to uproot a tree stump with their raw, bare hands.

A long-haired dachshund trotted by in a fetching plaid collar and matching tam-o'-shanter (Ivanito would've gladly snapped up the ensemble for himself). Nearby an elderberry bush unfurled its blossoming fans as brazenly as any burlesque queen. He knew the Tiergarten intimately: its meandering footpaths and hidden brambles (perfect for hookups); its ponds and glistening lakes; the often ribald nudists' meadow known as der Fleischweise.

A bearded young cub in tight jeans shot him a let's-fuck look but Ivanito was disinclined to frolic. In this, too, his mother had derailed him. The last thing he needed was for her to show up in the bushes while he was in flagrante delicto. When was the last time he'd had sex, anyway? Was it with that sullen leather daddy behind the Zoo Station? At the bathhouse off Nollendorfplatz? Shit, he couldn't remember.

Ivanito spied two women, identical twins—tall and lanky and vaguely familiar—sifting through an Ostalgie kiosk brimming with GDR memorabilia. They weren't beautiful but arresting, somehow. One was stylish in a teal jumpsuit, perfection from every angle. The other twin, rumpled in a Humboldt-Universität sweatshirt, wore outdated glasses that screamed East Germany. The country had vanished a decade ago but its detritus had become a jackpot for collectors, nostalgists, and the morbidly curious.

"I refuse to be anyone's poor Ossi mouse!" the rumpled one said, flushing with resentment. "We're not bargains to be snapped up by the likes of you!"

"You're hardly a bargain, Tereza."

"Richtig. Like that girl you picked up last night?"

The stylish twin didn't react except to step away from the kiosk and light a Cuban cigar, a Cohiba Espléndido, to be specific. The cigars weren't difficult to find—they were legal in Germany, after all—but this woman drew on hers like a connoisseur. Ivanito watched the smoke rise through the draping branches of a weeping willow.

Ivanito was tempted to approach these sisters, but to say what, exactly? *Excuse me—have we met before?* Compliment one on her outfit (and cigar choice)? Offer the other unsolicited sartorial advice? Just then, Azul raced over and climbed into his lap, waving an old VHS of *Some Like It Hot* dubbed in German. It was his favorite movie, he said, and Marilyn Monroe was his favorite actress. Natürlich.

"Listen to this!" Azul's face went earnestly blank for his Marilyn imitation. "Real diamonds!" he said breathlessly. "They must be worth their weight in gold!" Damn, if he wasn't convincing. Ivanito laughed, feeling an affinity with his nephew that went beyond the familial.

A flock of sparrows scattered off a beech tree. Ivanito searched for the twins again, but they were gone.

"Can we go to the zoo now, Tío?"

It was hard to deny this boy anything, but Ivanito was wary of stirring up Mami's ghost, much less another imbroglio with the German police. He suggested renting boats on the Neuer See, a safer choice. It would be lively with amateur rowers today, and Pilar, newly laden with crockery, was ready to go.

Ivanito Villaverde

Berlin

Their excursion to the Neuer See restored all three to some version of equilibrium after the morning's upheavals. They circumvented the bird sanctuary, where a goshawk guarded its nest high in a pine tree. Distracted by a falling chick—its mother swooped to the rescue— Ivanito collided with another boat. Apart from this mishap, he acquit-ted himself well as the rower-in-chief—oarlocks positioning was key—and the boat stayed balanced so long as Pilar and Azul remained seated in the stern. At one point Azul pretended to be a pirate, hold-ing up imaginary binoculars, and nearly tumbled into the water.

Back onshore the cousins settled under the Biergarten's chestnut trees and ate two loaded bockwursts apiece (Pilar had declared her-self a nonvegetarian while in Berlin). Ivanito taught his nephew to hum the opening melody to Beethoven's only violin concerto, argu-ably his most lyrical work. On the way home in the fading light, they stopped for ice cream near the opera house. Azul ordered for everyone in German: Zitrone for Pilar; Schokolade mit Himbeer for Ivanito; and Sahne-Kirsch for himself. Pilar marveled at her son's growing fluency, how intrepidly he navigated Berlin. But Ivanito wasn't surprised. Azul was lucky to have Pilar's patient, laissez-faire love. Not once had he heard her condescend to her son.

When Ivanito was a boy, his mother alternated between extremes of neglect and overprotection. She might leave him alone for days at a time, yet chastise him for using a butter knife to cut his food. And she was jealous of anyone—or anything—that came between them. When he fell in love with studying Russian, he had to hide it from her: the language's lush, buzzing sounds; the majesty of his name in Cyrillic: Иван. With his teachers' support, Ivanito won a summer scholarship to St. Petersburg but Mami refused to let him go. It took him many years to resume his Russian studies, this time at Moscow State Linguistic University.

As the trio approached Ivanito's apartment, ice cream nearly finished, Ivanito blinked, stunned to see the very same twins from the flea market now leaning against a cream-colored Trabi.

"You must be Ivanito," the stylish one said in Russian, extending her hand. "My father and your mother were brother and sister." She offered him a shopping bag from the specialty food department of KaDeWe. "Some caviar for our reunion, dear cousin."

Ivanito froze to the spot, staring at the sisters in disbelief. Were these "cousins" emissaries from his mother? More evidence of her scheming?

"I'm not sure what's going on," Pilar said into the awkward silence. "But maybe we can find a common language? How about English, or español?"

"They're our cousins, Mom," Azul whispered, having understood the Russian.

"Big happiness to meet you," the stylish cousin said in halting English.

Her disheveled sister's English was textbook-precise: "We are deeply heartened to make your acquaintance."

Azul wriggled between the two, charming them with his flourishing German. "Ihr beide seid wunderschön." What a little Lothario! A delighted Irina kissed Azul's cheek and showed him how to whistle like a Muscovite. The shrillness made Ivanito's halo wrench painfully counterclockwise.

"Can we invite you upstairs?" Pilar asked, directing a what-the-fuck's-wrong-with-you look at Ivanito.

"Forgive my manners, but I saw you both at the Flohmarkt this afternoon." Ivanito's halo felt like a thirty-kilo helmet. His speech began accelerating in fits and starts until he became a one-man Tower of Babel spewing a hodgepodge of Russian, German, English, and Spanish. Was this some kind of psycholinguistic breakdown? A synaptic misfiring?

Azul saved the day by pulling his uncle down to eye level and jamming the last of his cherry ice cream cone on his head. Only then did Ivanito's delirium stop. He regained his composure and invited his astonished new cousins upstairs.

Irina made herself instantly at home, taking command. She rattled through the tiny kitchen's drawers, set dishes and glasses on the living room coffee table, and enlisted Azul to unpack her mother-of-pearl spoons for the caviar.

"What's caviar?" he asked.

"Fish eggs," she explained.

Azul looked stricken. "I'm almost vegetarian," he declared, and everyone laughed.

Ivanito and Pilar were impressed by the munificent feast: multiple tins of chilled ossetra caviar (with accompaniments); a rosy slab of smoked salmon; and eight bottles of top-notch vodka, several of which Irina slid into the freezer to chill. She piled toast points high with caviar and crème fraîche and distributed them all around. Ivanito had never tasted anything so delicious. There was kovrizhka with nuts for dessert. Where had Irina found a Russian honey cake in Berlin?

Earlier that spring, the sisters explained, they'd run across each other at a queer tango dance along the Spree River. Evidently, they'd been separated at birth in Prague, then raised a thousand miles apart in Moscow and East Berlin. They said this as matter-of-factly as they might have described the weather.

"But how did that happen?" Pilar asked.

"We can't tell you what we don't know," Tereza said. "Except that our reunion was quite accidental. We're still trying to figure it out."

"We visit Mutti in nursing home but she say nothing."

"My mother is very ill," Tereza explained, glaring at her sister. "I don't know what she remembers. I don't think *she* knows what she remembers."

"Like criminal forget crime!"

"That's not fair!"

"Decide for self." Irina passed around a photograph of her father, Javier del Pino, holding her as an infant.

Ivanito recognized him at once: the handsome, drunken uncle who'd returned home after studying abroad. Tío Javier used to swim so far out to sea that everyone feared he was determined to drown. Later, it was rumored that he'd hanged himself from a giant ceiba tree on the carnival route in Santiago de Cuba. Nobody knew for sure. Somehow, for the first time, it occurred to Ivanito that he'd grown up in a matriarchy, where boys became men who lost their way while the women soldiered on.

"We're products of the Cold War," Tereza said, nervously slicing the air. "Products of its distortions, its lies."

"You can't whitewash your mother's deception." Irina reverted to Russian.

"No one person is to blame."

"We're talking about our lives here!"

"The political and the personal are inseparable," Ivanito interjected, hoping to establish common ground. Hadn't all of them been torn up by their roots? Their lives misshapen by one upheaval or another: revolution, immigration, dislocation? Ivanito had grown up navigating Abuela Celia's die-hard Communism, Mami's political shiftlessness, and Tía Lourdes's hard-core capitalism. By his mid-twenties, he'd lived in four countries and had visited many more. Emboldened by a second shot of vodka, he asked: "So, which political system do you think is the worst?"

The cousins began talking all at once, but Irina's voice rose above the rest. In her fervor, she switched to Russian entirely, grateful to let Ivanito translate for her. She launched into an unsparing attack against Stalin—his show trials and gulags, his starvation of millions of Ukrainian peasants, the Great Terror of the 1930s. When his own son was captured by the Germans in World War II, Stalin let him languish at Sachsenhausen—the concentration camp outside Berlin—until his death two years later.

Irina continued with a defense of the post-Soviet economy, while insisting she was decidedly more pragmatic than political. "At least we don't stand in line for hours anymore. Or bow to the mindless functionaries who ruled our lives. Voobshche." She stretched her shoulders, popping her joints as if preparing to lift a barbell. "And I became an entrepreneur—a very rich one. What's freedom, if not that?"

"Money isn't everything," Tereza shot back. "And flaunting yours is sehr geschmacklos. Besides, relatively few Russians are prospering and almost all by illegal means."

"But in a free market—"

"The free market isn't free!" Tereza launched into a tirade about the backroom privatizing deals that had sent East German unemployment soaring, all under the guise of winding down its inefficient economy. Eine Schande!

Ivanito couldn't tell if the twins were the best of friends, or mortal enemies. They were certainly trading barbs like live munitions. The sisters, he suspected, might be a living dialectic, a desperate, flesh-and-blood attempt at reconciliation. Pilar had trouble keeping up with the linguistic mix-and-match, but when she offered to tell the sisters about their grandmother, they stopped bickering.

Abuela Celia, she said, had fallen in love with a married Spanish lawyer who abandoned her in Havana in 1934. On the rebound, she married a straitlaced traveling salesman, Jorge del Pino, whom she never loved. For twenty-five years Celia wrote to her Spaniard but never sent the letters—except for the first one, which she'd committed to memory: *November 11, 1934. Mi querido Gustavo, A fish swims in my lung. Without you, what is there to celebrate?*

"Later, Abuela found her true purpose in the Revolution," Pilar went on. "And she fell in love again—with El Líder."

"That old goat?" Irina scoffed. "I was already sick of him as a schoolgirl!"

"He was a very romantic hero in the GDR," Tereza sighed. "That untamed beard, his sexy cigar. All the boys wanted to be like him. He was so *un*-German."

They all laughed, dispelling the sisters' tension.

Ivanito wondered what their grandmother would make of them today. These Cuban-Czech twins, as opposite politically as they were physically identical. Azul, her adorable Cuban-Japanese great-grandson. The middle-aged Pilar, whom Abuela had accused of being a traitor for helping Ivanito leave the island. And he himself, her polyglot drag queen of a grandson, whom she also hadn't forgiven for abandoning her and the Revolution.

"What happened to the letters?" Tereza asked, ever the archivist.

"She gave them to me." What Pilar didn't say was that afterward Abuela never spoke to her again.

"Our grandmother was also a decent pianist." Ivanito said, putting Debussy's "La Soirée dans Grenade" on the turntable. "She nearly wore out the keys with this one." There was a world of wounded eroticism in her playing, never so much as on the days when the sea was rough and the royal palms bowed in the winds.

Irina pulled a Cohiba from her pocket and leaned out a living room window, smoking into the night. Then, as if she'd been considering the idea for months, she announced: "We'll go to Cuba this summer!" She grabbed her cell phone and called her travel agent. She seemed intent on bankrolling a family trip on the spot.

Irina was charismatic, a natural saleswoman, but Ivanito had no desire to set foot on the island again. For what? To go courting the wretchedness of his past? Bumping into memories he'd sooner forget? If he missed anything about Cuba, it was its tropical vegetation, the turbulence of its skies.

"How about your mother?" Irina, on hold, asked Pilar. "Could she tell us more?"

Pilar let out a protracted sigh. "I doubt she'd be helpful."

"Why not?"

"Because she's incapable of telling the truth about anything. Besides, she left Cuba when Tío Javier was only a teenager."

Ivanito could tell that Pilar felt cornered. Did Irina actually think she could bulldoze them into ersatz solidarity overnight? Herd them into unwanted obligations? He was inclined to help her, certainly, but he refused to submit to some lurching, roots-seeking odyssey. It had taken every ounce of his strength to leave Cuba in the first place.

"How about fourth July?" Irina asked them.

"I don't want to go back." Ivanito was resolute.

"Me, neither," Pilar added sullenly.

"I'll go!" Azul slid next to Irina.

"Of course, Little Fish," Irina said, smoothing his hair. "We go first-class."

"It's a very generous offer." Ivanito hesitated before continuing. "But let's just say there are ghosts we don't want to stir up."

"Prizraki?" Irina looked skeptical.

Ivanito nodded.

"I might consider going," Tereza said quietly, "if you promise to leave Mutti alone."

"I don't think that's—"

"That's what's on offer, Irina. Take it or leave it."

Irina turned to Azul. "What do you think, Little Fish?"

"Deal!" he barked. "Take it!"

"You don't negotiate? Ah, we have much work to do!"

Irina ended the call and poured another round of vodka shots.

She seemed resigned to back off from the trip to Havana, at least for now.

"Cheers!" She held up her glass, and everyone followed suit.

The cousins huddled together in the living room and toasted one another ever more drunkenly as the night wore on. Azul, wrapped in his ostrich-feather boa, merrily drank along with a mug of Apfelsaft. *To our lost tribe! To our reunion! To our size-ten feet!* At one point they removed their shoes and marveled at their identical toes—even Azul's, in miniature. Tereza loved hearing about Pilar and Ivanito's punk days and promised to take them to the Garage Band Club in Treptower, where they could show off their chops.

"Believe me, we weren't very good," Pilar said. "That's sort of the point with punk. That anybody with a little energy and attitude can take the stage."

"We had that, all right!" Ivanito bellowed, downing another shot.

Nobody was in a hurry to separate. The more vodka they drank, the more stories they told. Irina recounted how in her crowded communal apartment in Moscow ("Only nine square meters of living space per person!"), the children liked to play dress-up with dead-drunk Uncle Fyodor in the hallway. Ivanito repeated his first raspy words in English, direct from Wolfman Jack's radio show: *You thought she was diggin' you but she was diggin' me!* Tereza confessed to her crush on John Travolta, whose smoldering photo—passed around like pornography—appeared in a contraband teen magazine from the West. And Pilar told how she'd painted a mural of the Statue of Liberty—with a safety pin through her nose—for her mother's second Yankee Doodle Bakery in Brooklyn.

When the caviar and salmon ran out, Ivanito ordered in sausage pizzas. They devoured those in no time. For dessert he served plums, defrosted cream puffs, and a half-eaten box of Belgian chocolates. When Tereza turned on the TV for the midnight news report, they learned that Bertha, the missing polar bear, had been found dead on the grounds of the German-Russian Museum in Karlshorst. There were no updates on her keeper, though he was believed to be at large in Ukraine.

"Who killed her?" Azul burst into tears.

"We don't know that anyone killed her," Pilar said, gently adjusting her son's ostrich-feather boa and cradling him in her arms. But the boy was inconsolable. Ivanito watched the tenderness between them. Here was a child who trusted the gift of his mother's solace. At last Azul fell asleep, and Pilar tucked him into bed clutching his soggy boa.

Ivanito offered to let the twins sleep off the vodka at his place and they gratefully accepted. Tereza slumped on the worn burgundy sofa while Irina leaned back in the Breuer chaise longue and closed her eyes. Soon both of them were tenderly snoring. A whimpering Pilar, unaccustomed to 100-proof vodka, collapsed face-forward on the rug and drooled. Only Ivanito stayed awake, gazing out the windows. A half-moon lingered in the western skies, faint and benign.

For once he had no presentiment of disaster. Perhaps he might even rest.

MIAMI-HAVANA

I

⚘

Lourdes Puente

Miami

An ON AIR sign lights up inside a radio station in Miami.

RADIO HOST: This is *Cafecito con Paquito* at Radio Mambí, WAQI 710 on your AM dial, bringing Miami Cubans *our* news! Today, we have as our special guest the fast-rising political star Lourdes Puente. She's shaken up the establishment by announcing her run for Miami-Dade mayor in the upcoming November elections. Bienvenida, Lourdes.

LOURDES: Un placer, Paquito.

RADIO HOST: Please tell the listeners of *Cafecito con Paquito* why you decided to challenge Alex Panetela, un demócrata, for the top seat in the county.

LOURDES: As you know, Paquito, I've been very involved in the tragic case of Eliseo González. Mayor Panetela, for all his bluster, did nothing to stop the deportation of our innocent boy back to the tyranny of Cuba. He should have done better! And I *will* do better to make sure que una barbaridad like that won't happen again!

RADIO HOST: I know our listeners share your passion, Lourdes.

LOURDES: Mayor Panetela claims to be a moderate but we know what that means: he's un comunista, pure and simple! Who can be a moderate when it comes to protecting our children, eh? It's a contradiction in terms.

RADIO HOST: Bien dicho, Lourdes. Before we continue, let's take a short break for our number-one sponsor, La Cuba Libre Bakery, serving the freshest pastelitos de guayaba in Hialeah!

VOICEOVER: *¿Quinceañera? ¿Aniversario? ¿El bautismo de tu nieto? La Cuba Libre Bakery is famous for its custom-made cakes con el sabor de la isla . . . We deliver!*

RADIO HOST: If you're just tuning in, this is *Cafecito con Paquito* at Radio Mambí, WAQI 710 on your AM dial. We're speaking to Lourdes Puente, the firebrand challenger to Alex Panetela in the Miami-Dade mayor's race. So, tell us, Lourdes, how do you respond to critics who say you have no political experience?

LOURDES: Primero, I'm a businesswoman, an entrepreneur, an immigrant success story. I ran two very profitable bakeries in Brooklyn for over twenty years. Créame, that prepares you for anything. Being mayor would be a *piece of cake* compared to that!

RADIO HOST: ¡Jajaja! A politician with a sense of humor. ¡Qué tremenda! Now let's open the phone lines to callers. Our toll-free number is 1-ABAJOFIDEL. From North Miami Beach, Mimí Peña, you're on the air.

CALLER #1: Hola. I want to thank Lourdes for her service.

RADIO HOST: Perdóneme, Mimí, but Lourdes wasn't in the military.

LOURDES: Mimí means for all I did to try to keep Eliseo in Miami. ¿No es cierto, Mimí?

CALLER #1: Así mismo. Gracias, Lourdes.

LOURDES: De nada, Mimí. And with the blessing of La Virgen de la Caridad del Cobre, you can expect me to do mucho más as mayor of Miami-Dade. Too many americanos don't understand the suffering of the Cuban people at the hands of those blood-thirsty comunistas for over forty years! Y no se olvide what happened at the Bay of Pigs!

RADIO HOST: Bebo García calling from Fort Lauderdale. You're on the air.

CALLER #2: I retired up the coast to get away from the crime in Miami—especially from those Marielito delincuentes. El Líder emptied his prisons and sent all the criminals here!

RADIO HOST: What's your question, Bebo?

CALLER #2: I want to know, Lourdes, what you plan to do about the skyrocketing murder rate.

LOURDES: I'm glad you asked, Bebo. As a former auxiliary police-woman, I have a history in law enforcement. And I am proposing a *zero tolerance* policy for crime. If I'm elected mayor of Miami-Dade, all perpetrators will be prosecuted to the fullest extent of the law—including the death penalty.

RADIO HOST: ¡Ñoo! The phones are ringing off the hook! From Kendall, you're on the air.

CALLER #3: You've been in Miami less than ten years. What makes you think that you—a carpetbagger—can run a county you hardly know?

LOURDES: ¿Una *qué*? I sold pastries, not rugs.

CALLER #3: And there's such a thing as separation of church and state in the U.S.

LOURDES: Who are you, anyway?

CALLER #3: The question is: Who are *you*, Lourdes Puente?

Sound of telephone click. Radio Host and Lourdes exchange dubious looks.

LOURDES: ¡Qué paquete, Paquito!

RADIO HOST: We'll be taking more calls after a word from our sponsor: Caimán Automotive Repairs. From Jaguars to cacha-rros, Caimán fixes them all!

VOICEOVER: *Having car trouble? El Caimán Automotive Repairs "snaps to" when it comes to your ride. Trust El Caimán.* [Sound of alligator roar.]

RADIO HOST: We're back! This is *Cafecito con Paquito* at Radio Mambí, WAQI 710 AM. Don't you dare turn that dial, compays! Again, our toll-free number is 1-ABAJOFIDEL. Pues, Lourdes, there are those who accuse you of not paying your dues, of not putting in your time.

LOURDES: My time is now, Paquito. I don't have to do this. I'm retired, a wealthy woman. But la desgracia of the Eliseo affair calls for new energy, new blood, an iron commitment to freedom and democracy. That this outrage could've happened right here in Miami is . . . is outrageous! This is America, not Communist Cuba!

RADIO HOST: Welcome, Rick Andrews from Liberty City. You're on the air.

CALLER #4: As an African American and a member of the Miami community, I was in favor of sending Eliseo back to his father in Cuba. It's where he belongs.

LOURDES: Mr. Andrews, have you ever been to Cuba?

CALLER #4: I don't see what that has to do—

LOURDES: Because if you knew that island-prison firsthand, you couldn't send a child back there. That's all I'm going to say to you right now.

RADIO HOST: We have a long-distance call from Berlin, Germany. ¡Mira pa' eso! We're a global station now! Go ahead, you're on the air.

CALLER #5: Mom, what the hell are you doing? Are you out of your mind?

LOURDES: Ah, so you finally call me, only to make a spectacle of yourself?

PILAR: You're the one who's making a spectacle of yourself! It's bad enough you nearly killed Azul, and didn't even bother to apologize—

RADIO HOST: Who's Azul?

LOURDES (*sotto voce*): My grandson.

RADIO HOST: You almost killed him?

LOURDES: ¡Claro que no! Who do you think I am?

PILAR: And now you're trying to inflict your deranged ideas on all of South Florida?

LOURDES: I have a great deal of support from el pueblo here!

PILAR: Oh, spare me your "el pueblo" [BEEP]. You don't give a [BEEP] about "el pueblo" unless you can get them to work for you at below minimum wage.

LOURDES: And I was jailed for my beliefs!

PILAR: A bathroom break at the police station doesn't count as jail time. To everyone listening: DON'T VOTE FOR MY MOTHER! SHE'S A SHILL FOR THE REPUBLICANS!

LOURDES: CUT HER OFF! CUT HER OFF!

PILAR: TAKE MY WORD FOR IT! YOU'LL REGRET—

Pilar is cut off.

LOURDES: ¡SINVERGÜENZA!

RADIO HOST *(nonplussed)*: You're listening to *Cafecito con Paquito* at Radio Mambí, WAQI 710 AM, bringing Miami Cubans our news! And now a word from a very special sponsor, Cuerpo de Cuba Beauty Supplies, in Coral Gables.

VOICEOVER: *Time may be indifferent, but you needn't be! Cuerpo de Cuba Beauty Supplies will keep you alluring forever. . . . Visit us at our store on Miracle Mile and discover your very own fountain of youth. . . . Senior discounts available seven days a week!*

2

Luz and Milagro Villaverde

Miami

Milagro and I started talking about moving north, to where we didn't have to pretend to belong. Nothing was worse—more *nowhere*—than being an exile within the exile. We were pushing forty, too, with no suitors in sight. Babies flying on our radars like mangoes in a hurricane. They were everywhere: in supermarkets, strollers, under the beach umbrellas at Crandon Park. That was when we decided to try to have a baby of our own—but without the local species of strutting rooster.

So, in the middle of all this, who did we run into at Parrot Jungle? Eusebio Delgado, the younger son of Herminia, our mother's best friend. Y qué guapetón—with muscles to the moon! He told us that he sailed from Cuba to Florida last year on a boat he'd built himself. I might've gone for Eusebio myself but it didn't take long for Milagro and him to fall crazily in love. Seriously arrebatados. I was jealous for about a week. But I reminded myself that it was Milagro who was in love. My sister, my double helix. Her happiness was inextricable from my own. Ñoo, if she didn't get pregnant fast, too! It was like winning the Florida lottery, which was up to $17 million that week.

Yesterday we learned that Milagro was carrying a boy. "He's perfect," Dr. Obejas said. "Very healthy and growing well. Brain, heart, kidneys, limbs—all good." Eusebio cried like a baby himself when he heard the news and ran off to call his mother. Milagro left a message for our brother in Berlin. How would he react to becoming an uncle? Would Ivanito finally come visit us in Miami? Milagro was so hopeful that she decided to name the baby after him.

Of course, I was dead set against it. Abuela Celia had named our mother, Felicia, after una loca in the asylum who'd set her husband on fire. Names were destiny, I said. So, why pick one with a history of suffering?

3

Herminia Delgado

Santa Teresa del Mar

This morning Eusebio called to tell me I was going to be a grand-mother. ¡Qué emoción! Claro, I hurried off to the cemetery to give Felicia the news. I brought along a broom and fresh cuttings from Celia's garden: bird-of-paradise, hibiscus, gardenias. I swept Felicia's grave, wiped off her headstone, laid the flowers where I imagined her heart would be.

"Perdóname, Felicia. It's been months, I know. But wait until I tell you why!"

I gave her a moment to respond but she said nothing.

"Can you send me a sign that you hear me? It's important!"

More silence.

"Don't go playing hide-and-seek with me, chica. This has to do with our children!"

Just as I was losing my patience, a blue-headed quail dove landed on her headstone, then fluttered to the ground and stared at me. Bueno, if this was the best Felicia could do, I should at least have the good grace to accept it.

"Óyeme, Eusebio and Milagro are in love! They're going to have a baby!"

The dove cocked its head and puffed up its chest, its cobalt crown shiny in the sun. It circled in place, round and round, making me dizzy.

"Sí, we're going to be abuelas! Remember that oath we took as girls? When we cut our thumbs and vowed to be friends forever?"

The dove hopped into my lap and buried its head against my belly, cooing and letting me caress its feathers. What could I say? There were answers when we looked for them. And the dead? Bueno, ya tú sabes, they're never entirely dead.

INTERLUDE: PILAR'S PHOTOS

Image #5: 1980

It's Thanksgiving Day, my least favorite holiday—a.k.a. National Day of Mourning. My mother and I sit opposite each other at the dining room table. There's a Cuban feast between us: roast pork, congrí, fried plantains, croqueticas de jamón, yuca con mojo, avocado salad, buñuelos for dessert. No colossal dried-out turkey for us. Ivanito is next to me, freshly kidnapped from Cuba. Mom is leaning toward him, her mouth open, her look intense.

Poor Ivanito is shell-shocked from his move to Brooklyn. Most days he just stares for hours at the withering elm tree in our backyard. Maybe he's thinking of his mother, Tía Felicia, who died the previous spring. Everyone argues over whether Tía Felicia killed herself, or died from grief. What does it matter? Ivanito lost his mother and his country in one fell swoop. Shouldn't time stop for that?

Mom thinks she can make Ivanito forget the past by disparaging everything he loves. He's fluent in Russian and was a star pupil back in Cuba, winning the Vladimir Lenin Gold Star for his age group three years in a row. Mom doesn't know the first thing about Russian culture, literature, history—or cosmonauts, for that matter. To her, the USSR is the vilest of empires, the epicenter of Communism, the derailer of Cuba's fate and, most important, her own.

"Hard work will fix your leftist depression, Ivanito." Mom is determined to root out any vestigial brainwashing in him. "This is your chance at the American dream!"

Right. Like working at her bakeries, for free, will be his salvation.

My cousin slips in and out of what I consider his fugue states. His teachers call, worried about his mental health. They report that Ivanito can't focus on his schoolwork, throws his lunch in the trash, drinks nothing but Coca-Cola. At Mom's bakeries he ignores the customers, or forgets to charge them. Sometimes he gives away sticky buns, her bestseller.

This infuriates Mom. She can't begin to see his trauma through the cataracts of her own.

"What right do you have to give away what's mine?" That's what she's saying to him at Thanksgiving dinner when Dad takes our picture. Dad's cooked the banquet himself. His toque is askew, his elbow bandaged, his apron filthy from days in the kitchen. It makes me wonder if what we don't see is actually more important than what we do.

Image #6: 1984

Ivanito and I are at CBGB's, stoned out of our minds. We're draped over each other, a molten, happy mess of vodka and speed. Who the hell knows who took this Polaroid? Me in my skinny black jeans and studded leather jacket; Ivanito, his hair bleached to oblivion, looking ethereal, nearly transparent except for his eyes, a camera-flash red. Graffiti and shredded flyers are plastered on the wall behind us. We have lots of nights like this one.

I'm the bassist for my punk band, Autopsy. Ivanito is just finishing high school, a lamb I'm making it my business to corrupt. He's our band's jailbait lead singer, ushering us to our nanosecond of downtown fame. To Mom's horror, Ivanito skipped the confused-sexuality phase altogether and came out with a vengeance at fifteen.

Naturally, she blamed me for "feminizing" him.

Not long after this picture was taken, the punk movement fell apart—and AIDS raged on for years. Generations of artists and renegades were brutally wiped out. Our lexicon was forced to adapt to the raw reality of T-cell counts, Kaposi's sarcoma, retinitis, viral loads. Ivanito lost four close friends to the decimation. "Only four?" people asked him incredulously. By the standards of the day, he was astoundingly lucky.

My cousin and I are eight years apart but we were very close for a time. We got our noses pierced, had matching scorpions tattooed on our wrists, confided in each other over love gone raucously bad. Nothing mattered more to us than the elation of the moment. It makes me happy and unbearably sad to look at this photograph, to remember our freedom and recklessness, our flying off every cliff without batting an eye.

How I miss those days when we lived, briefly, as one.

IV

BERLIN-GRANADA

In which the tango seduces him on a Berlin rooftop . . .

The tango party took place every Thursday on a rooftop in Wilmersdorf, weather permitting. It featured a live trio with a superb bandoneon player from Buenos Aires, grilled steak-and-chimichurri sandwiches, and an abundance of Mendoza wines. Tereza swore that it was the friendliest milonga in the city—families, queers, and beginners were all welcome—though professional dancers often joined the festivities as the night wore on. She'd been lobbying for the cousins to give tango a try. Tonight, Tereza was getting her wish.

It was the middle of a very rainy June. The five of them had been inseparable for weeks, gathering at Ivanito's place every evening. They switched from English (their "common" language) to German and Russian, with interjections of Spanish (expletives, mostly). They told and retold their stories, succumbing to a wilderness of what-ifs. Irina was managing her lingerie empire from the factory in Berlin and kept a suite at the Hotel Adlon. She took pleasure in supplying their daily feasts. For supper she'd brought over a roast pork shoulder, parsley potatoes, white asparagus in peppered butter sauce, and pot de crème for dessert.

Who could think of dancing after a meal like that?

Ivanito's apartment was, as usual, a shambles. Dishes of leftovers were strewn alongside high heels, backpacks, dirty socks, broken pottery, and fencing gear. Irina had bought Azul a set of half-size swords and was giving him lessons. "En garde, Little Fish! You go nowhere without killer instinct! Bud' gotov!" Azul fought with a stubborn intensity. Pilar had still another cause for surprise about her own son: Who knew he was so competitive? During breaks in the fencing, Irina and Tereza heatedly argued over politics.

Meanwhile Pilar had converted Ivanito's second bedroom into a makeshift art studio—she was on a tear with her kintsugi experiments—and had maimed his birch desk, a vintage geometric rug, and fistfuls of kitchen implements. Lately, she'd taken to repairing broken porcelain teacups with tiny rubber-padded clamps and her noxious gold-dust epoxy. More interesting to Ivanito was her series of pencil-thin, gravity-defying totemic sculptures (beautiful and mysterious), which she assembled from her piles of mismatched pottery shards.

At the moment, Pilar was focused on fixing the broken mirror of his antique mahogany armoire from Havana. Azul claimed that he'd been watching a pair of old-fashioned lovebirds dancing inside the mirror—"like in a movie"—when it inexplicably cracked, as if by a slingshot's rock. Pilar shrugged off the incident, but Ivanito understood it as further proof that he and Azul shared a gift for the otherworldly, for seeing what others could not.

Unfortunately, the chronic domestic anarchy kept triggering his halo. It was staticky at all hours now, like his old shortwave radio in Cuba, and Ivanito half expected to hear Wolfman Jack howling in his ears. Mornings, especially, the halo issued a grating whine, as if it were sharpening knives in its spare time. Not to mention the recurring migraines the accursed thing induced. It was a reminder to him that he was in a battle of wills with his dead mother, with the seduction of death itself.

Tonight Ivanito was helping his cousins dress for the tango party. If it was a bust, at least they would all look fabulous. The tuxedo he lent Tereza fit her perfectly, transforming her into a *GQ* model—the sisters were five-eleven—and hiding her jungle armpits. The chic—and depilated—Irina slipped into a haltered, leopard-print bodysuit that showed off her lady-killer rhomboids. He'd heard through the grapevine that his cousin, a.k.a. "Die Wow-Russin," was the hottest newcomer to Berlin's lesbian scene.

Pilar, unsurprisingly, was a nightmare to dress. Eschewing his advice, she put together an ensemble consisting of a top hat, fishnet stockings, and Lederhosen, which Ivanito charitably dubbed "neo-Bavarian strumpet." Azul looked handsome in a shrunken Nehru jacket (another flea-market find) and a pair of round, orange-tinted sunglasses—a baby John Lennon. Ivanito himself metamorphosed into a showstopping Evita Perón: platinum pompadour, carmine-red lipstick, and a forties strapless taffeta. Bring on that Casa Rosada balcony!

Together the five of them piled into Tereza's rattletrap Trabi, windows down, for the short drive to Wilmersdorf. The night was warm, saturated with the blooming chestnut trees' semeny scent. And the Trabi, with its two-stroke lawn mower engine, sputtered and smoked as it rolled through the streets of Charlottenburg. It was by far the worst car ever built, no matter its rising cult status.

En route Irina provoked her sister into another round of sniping.

"How about we pay your mother a visit instead of going tango dancing?"

"Not happening," Tereza snapped.

"How else will we get to the bottom of her deceit?"

"Don't think you can control me, Irina. Much less everyone else."

"Excuse me," Azul interrupted. "Do I have an extra grandmother?"

"Your babushka is big thief!" Irina blurted in English.

"How dare you?" Tereza screeched to a halt in the middle of Kantstrasse. Around them drivers honked and cursed. Tereza only gripped the steering wheel harder.

"Uh, maybe you should pull over?" Pilar suggested.

"Watch that truck!" Ivanito shrieked.

"If you don't come with me to Cuba," Irina threatened, "I swear I'll go straight to her verdammter nursing home and—"

"Okay."

"What?"

"I said okay, Irina. I'll go with you to Cuba if it means that much to you."

"Really?"

"Ja. Mutti's health permitting."

Irina opened her mouth, then shut it. And just like that, their argument deflated.

"Es ist ein Wunder!" Azul cheered.

"About fucking time," Ivanito muttered, blotting his lipstick.

When they stopped at the next traffic light, a scowling pensioner shouted about lunatics overrunning Berlin since reunification.

The cousins rode up to the rooftop party in a creaky service elevator. Nine stories over the city's leafy flatlands was a romantic aerie, ablaze with candles and espaliered plum trees. A massive barbecue sizzled with skirt steaks. Splendently dressed couples, most same-sex, swirled counterclockwise to Piazzolla's infamous "Balada para un Loco." Ivanito-as-Evita caused a sensation on the arm of Tereza, a beloved local tango star.

Many tangueros recognized the twins from the early-spring dance along the Spree and begged them to perform together again. Who on the European queer tango circuit hadn't heard about their dramatic reunion? Tereza and Irina took their places at the center of the dance floor as the band struck up "Por una Cabeza." But to everyone's astonishment, the sisters' phrasing faltered and their bodies contradicted each other at every turn. They looked more like sparring partners than doppelgängers.

"Get out of your head," Tereza whispered. "Follow my lead." But Irina could barely execute a simple ocho. Frustrated, she stormed off and turned her back on the disappointed crowd. Staring angrily out toward the city beneath them, she lit a Cohiba to calm down.

With a dignity befitting the former first lady of Argentina, Evita took Irina's place. The cousins danced with ease, torsos aligned and provocatively off-axis, steps crisp and synchronous. As their confidence grew, they added crowd-pleasing firuletes, tijeras, and whipping boleos that incited a smattering of cheers. *Llorar, / llorar por una mujer / es quererla / y no tenerla. . . .* What was tango, if not embracing love and suffering in equal measure?

As Tereza dipped Ivanito in a flamboyant finale, he caught sight of Azul demonstrating a basic box step to Pilar near the edge of the roof. Incredibly, his own mother hovered high above them, looking like a Stygian owl—except she was spectrally white to the tips of her wings and flanked by a pair of giant doves. This was too fucking much! Was Mami scheming to swoop down on Azul like a bird of prey? Carry the boy off in her talons? ¿Cómo se atreve?

It took all of Ivanito's self-control to cursorily acknowledge the crowd's ovation. He had no time to waste on accolades. His mother floated in the roseate twilight, casting an expanding shadow on the roof, her face motionless, her wingbeats steady. The temperature dropped ten degrees. Then, stretching out one tufted leg, Mami released a glinting disk that spiraled toward Azul.

"Stop!" Ivanito screamed.

Everyone on the rooftop froze, as if suspended in time. Only he and the shivering Azul were moving. Mami coyly waved at the boy. Her blanched feathers rippled, though the air was perfectly still. The doves were suspended beside her like bodyguards. Chin uptilted, a spellbound Azul watched the halo slowly descend.

"Un regalito para ti, mi cielo." Mami's beak moved elastically, enunciating each word.

Azul stretched his arms toward the spiraling gold. ¡Carajo! Was he rising off the roof like La Asunción de María? Ivanito lunged for the boy, seizing him by the waist. Together they toppled against the parapet, nearly dropping the nine flights down. Ivanito feared that Mami might still abduct them both, broken-boned or not. He'd fight her to the bitter end, if necessary. But when he looked up again, she'd vanished.

Movement resumed on the dance floor.

"What the fuck's wrong with you?" Pilar said, grabbing her son.

Azul sniffled. He'd hit his head in the fall and a drip of blood stippled his cheek.

"Where is it, Tía?" he asked Ivanito, patting his head. "I don't feel it."

"I'm sorry, conejito. I was afraid—"

"But I wanted one, just like yours!"

"Wanted what?" Pilar asked.

"A halo!" Azul cried.

Ivanito faced the emptiness where his mother had been. The sky had a thousand invisible exits—panicked moon, black planets, its vault of stars. How could he possibly know where she'd gone? He scoured the rooftop in case Mami was lurking like a rogue angel somewhere, outwaiting his vigilance. There was no sign of her among the plum trees, where a morose Irina stood drinking malbec straight from a bottle.

Carefully, Ivanito scanned the horizon like Abuela Celia used to do when she'd guarded her stretch of Cuban coast. But he didn't spy so much as a crow.

A bit of smeared mascara blurred the vision in his left eye. Ivanito tried to blink it away. Would his mother dare lure Azul to his death with favors and promises, like she'd attempted with him at the same tender age? Did she really expect to get a second chance? How tired he was of her martyrdoms! Her eternal hungers! Would she ever stop haunting him? Settle down like an ordinary ghost in this capital of ghosts? Quietly return to her grave on the outskirts of Santa Teresa del Mar? Leave him, finally, in peace?

He doubted it.

Postscript

I almost lost my boy last night on a rooftop in Berlin. Azul wasn't hurt, but my heart got stuck in my throat. It was nobody's fault, really. The dead call on the living all the time.

Why did I pretend that nothing would change when I became a mother? Shouldn't everything change for a child? Was this what I'd blindly sought in Berlin: the privilege of stasis, of repair?

I had a boy with me here on earth, who was growing in the loam of my presence. Our love was expanding, inventively, in fits and starts. In the end he would leave me, as he should.

To accept this was a radical act.

Celia del Pino

In which the lovers dine together, accompanied by a flamenco trio . . .

"I dreamt that you'd return to me by sea." Celia held out her glass for more sherry.

"Like Christopher Columbus?"

"Sí, con la Niña, la Pinta, y la Santa María." She sang out the names like a schoolgirl.

"You see me as a conqueror, then?" Gustavo was a little too pleased with the analogy.

"You vanquished me long ago, mi amor." The candlelight became him, Celia thought. His features softened, blurred to a ruddy pink.

"I've asked your forgiveness but I know that's impossible."

"You don't need my forgiveness, Gustavo, and I don't need yours. If we begin with this sort of accounting, it will never end."

The waiters brought a platter of jamón serrano and a flurry of tapas—grilled shrimp, calamares fritos, chorizos, baby octopus, crabmeat croquettes, merluza a la romana, fresh anchovies, cod fritters, roasted peppers, fried salted almonds . . . it didn't stop!

Celia considered the feast, the empty restaurant. "Why are we the only ones here?"

"It's early yet," Gustavo said, though it was nearly midnight.

Celia had no idea what time it was in Santa Teresa del Mar. She'd never had to figure out time in relation to any other place before.

Time had been a constant on her beach, faster or slower only by her own subjective experience. Gustavo tempted Celia with a crabmeat croquette from the tip of his fork. She took a bite. Its creaminess disarmed her.

"You know, we didn't eat much at the Hotel Inglaterra." Gustavo offered her a morsel of chorizo flamed with brandy next. "I have a lot to make up for."

"Did you forget our arroz con cangrejos?" Celia succumbed to a nibble of merluza. "We devoured that every night."

With a slight tremor, Gustavo squeezed a few drops of lemon on a grilled shrimp and held it close to her lips. "I don't remember."

"And every morning, you heroically ventured out and brought us back mangoes and fruta bomba from a street vendor."

"Ah, that I do remember." Gustavo grinned, toying with a bit of fried squid.

"You ate the fruit right off my belly."

"And elsewhere, mi vida . . ."

"Say it, Gustavo. We're too old for euphemisms."

"Say what?" He feigned an innocent look.

"From where else you ate la fruta bomba."

"Eh . . . mmm . . ."

"Are you blushing, then?"

His face was as red as the roasted peppers. "I mix things up sometimes."

"¿A mí con ese cuento?" Celia laughed.

A trio of musicians set up on the restaurant's circular, elevated stage. There were two male guitarists, one with a full beard, and a striking, hook-nosed singer in a tight satin bodice and flamenco skirt, her hair twisted with high combs. With a nod from Gustavo, the guitarists began a cante jondo beloved by García Lorca.

"She's singing on my behalf," Gustavo murmured in Celia's ear. "From me to you."

The singer's voice cracked with heartbreak, radiating duende.

Once, Celia had imagined herself like this woman—the same stac-
cato of hands, her feet supple against the floorboards of the night,
a voluminous skirt glinting crimson.

Years ago, Pilar painted a portrait of Celia in a flamenco skirt
as she posed on her seaside porch. Her granddaughter had grown
enamored of the island's blues: the shoreline's aquamarines; its deep-
water azures; the midnight blues of the royal palms. And she managed to capture Celia's most intimate blues—the delicate indigos
beneath her eyes, the fading navy mole on her cheek.

A pair of waiters hauled in the seafood paella, enough for a small
wedding party.

"Are you sure you're not expecting anyone else?" Celia asked.

"Only you, mi reina."

The sommelier poured the wine, a Spanish albariño. Celia knew
nothing about wine except that she liked this one a lot. In Cuba,
only rum was widely available. She emptied her glass and Gustavo
refilled it.

"Despacio, corazón," he chided. "Let's keep our wits about us."

"Overrated." Celia drained the second glass.

"Then at least eat a little more." He added a dollop of paella to
her plate. "I want to hear everything about your life."

How irritating he was becoming, with this catching-up nonsense!
"There's not enough time to live it all over again," Celia snapped.

"I see. Then tell me about la revolución."

Celia felt stirred by the wine. "I would defend El Líder to his last
breath!" Just mentioning him made her crave a cigar.

"Which may be coming soon, no?"

"Are you mocking me?"

"Never."

Celia was riled up for a fight, but what would that solve? Their
last breaths, too, were coming soon. Why ruin the prelude? She
looked down at her plate. The paella, menos mal, was outstanding.

When was the last time she'd tasted saffron? If this were her final meal, she could die content.

Gustavo related, over dinner, how he'd been barred from practicing law following his imprisonment for political opposition during the Spanish Civil War. After his release, he taught at the University of Granada until his retirement fifteen years ago. "I was awarded the dubious prize of an academic position," he said. "I felt terribly broken, useless. But the students kept me going."

Between forkfuls of paella, Celia detailed her years as a civil judge in Santa Teresa del Mar. It had disheartened her to rule over petty cases—adulteries, score-settling between neighbors—none of which had any business before a judge. Twice she was forced to rule on cases involving her daughter, Felicia, despite the conflict of interest. Celia had a reputation for meting out creative sentences, like enrolling petty thieves in theater programs, or assigning an incorrigible Lothario to work at a baby nursery.

"So, we both partook of the law," Gustavo said, impressed.

"More like it partook of us!"

Inevitably, the conversation turned to their families. Gustavo lit up talking about his only daughter, Analise, who taught opera in Milan. She'd been a fine soprano in her day, he said, but not extraordinary enough to perform on the world's greatest stages. Analise never had children, though she'd been married briefly to a philandering cellist.

"We can't all be divas," Celia said softly. "Most of us resign ourselves to ceding the limelight to others."

Celia was reluctant to speak of her children: of Javier and Felicia, dead by their own hands; of Lourdes, long estranged by her reactionary politics. Some things were better left unsaid. Besides, what could she have offered in her own defense? That she'd been unfit for motherhood? That she'd never loved her husband? That only the Revolution, with its higher purpose, its lofty goals, had truly engaged her? That her grandchildren were scattered to the winds like rootless plants, without so much as an occasional word for her?

No, she wasn't inclined to speak about any of them.

"Family is not a happy topic for me, Gustavo." Celia feared destroying their present with laments from her past, though she knew she couldn't escape it entirely.

The seafood paella had grown cold in its vast, shallow pan. If only she could send the leftovers to Herminia, who'd devour it all in one sitting. Before she left Cuba, Celia had secretly bequeathed her little brick-and-cement house to her devoted neighbor.

"Why didn't you ever leave Spain?" Celia asked.

Gustavo stretched out his hand, a rosary of twisted bones, and stared at her. Was it admiration? Confusion? Love?

"For the same reasons you never left Cuba. It's your country, your patria. How could you abandon it in its hour of need?" He gripped her hand more urgently. "Exile is worse, much worse. Cowardly even. Don't you agree?"

"I thought so," Celia said, "until now."

"Have you abandoned your island, then?"

"Not yet, Gustavo. But I'm open to persuasion."

3

Ivanito Villaverde

In which he conjures his dead mother in the Tiergarten at dawn . . .

Ivanito walked into the Tiergarten early on summer solstice, not knowing if he would score a hookup, go swimming, or kill himself. Would he have to capitulate to his mother to save Azul? Was there no other way? Mami was maddening, impossible, vengeful. She would never submit to what she expected from him! Ivanito rambled across the Löwenbrucke, scanning the woods for sexual prospects, but there wasn't a soul around. Only the nightingales were singing up a storm, as their mating season waned. It was either too late, or too early, for cruising. He didn't look terribly appealing, either—unshaven, unwashed, unkempt.

A heron waded in the shallows of the Neuer See. Some dozen or so rowboats were moored to the freshly painted docks. Not long ago, Ivanito had gone boating here with Pilar and Azul. When was that, exactly? Time was increasingly unreliable, collapsing and eliding the present with the past. He yanked loose a rowboat, climbed aboard, and set it gliding across the lake. A brass-tinted moth with enormous brown eyespots flitted by.

Ivanito dropped an oar into the water and watched it slip under the algae. Was that the ripple of an eel? A breaching carp? He released the other oar. A pair of greylag geese appeared suspended in the skies, as if slackened by Venus's invisible forces. Why not float on this lake forever? Forget about steering his life in any particular direction? He was drifting on a boat in a man-made lake in the heart of Berlin. Maybe that was enough.

The rowboat got stuck in a clump of duckweed. As Ivanito wrested the boat free, he spotted a fox staring at him from shore. He searched its triangular face for a hint of what he should do. But the fox turned tail, disappearing into the forest once stocked with boar and deer for the Prussian aristocracy. Ivanito absently touched the mole on his cheek. He'd inherited it from his mother—and she, in turn, from Abuela Celia. The same beauty mark, marking them all, like a futile cause.

A bank of fog crept over the water's surface, thickening with buzzing insects. A dragonfly flew by, dispatching a wasp in midair. Abruptly, Ivanito stood in the rowboat and widened his stance until the rocking stopped. Could there ever be a rapprochement with his mother? A truce, however provisional? There was no denying that her love was flawed, but it had also been fiercely abundant.

The air grew humid with tropical sounds and fragrances. A sudden clamor of parrots. The aroma of butterfly jasmine wafting across the lake. A fury of liana and trumpet vines were overtaking the forest, choking off poplars and birches and pines. Close-packed jagüeys shot up fifty feet in the air, waving their vast, aerial roots. A flock of bullfinches darted from kapoks to cork palms, calling to one another with emphatic *tsi-tsi-tsis.*

Ivanito shook his head, but the visions persisted. Heliconias were twisting up everywhere, their lobster claws staging a horticultural coup of the Tiergarten. A bee hummingbird emerged out of the blue, whirring brightly. It flew in frantic loops, chirping and trilling, tiny wings ablur. Then it fluttered upward, a speck of color in the overcast skies, before plummeting headlong into the lake.

"¡Mami!" His voice echoed through the forest. "¡Aquí te espero!"

Ivanito thought of how he and his mother had clung to each other despite efforts by their family and the Revolution to pry them apart.

He pressed his palms together, as if in prayer. *Nothing should come between a mother and son. Nada en absoluto.*

"Mi cielo . . ." His mother's voice encircled his waist, a ribbon of warmth. Slowly, she appeared before him, youthful and happy, identical to the photograph he had of her on the beach in Santa Teresa del Mar.

"I see you," Ivanito said, surging with tenderness.

"Ay, niño mío . . ." His mother held his face gently, like an offering, and tilted it heavenward. Snow began to fall, lightly at first, then harder, swaddling them in waves of cold petals. His limbs stiffened, his lips went numb. The rapture of ice had arrived.

"I'll go with you," he said, yielding at last. "But leave Azul alone."

Mami drew his hands to her heart. Then she released them and peacefully vanished.

Overcome with drowsiness, Ivanito closed his eyes and jumped into the lake's glassy tranquility, succumbing to its blissful, enwombing silence.

When he dared look again, he was naked and floating on his back in the chilly waters, his hair loose, his legs relaxed and apart, his sex pinkly buoyant. The snow had stopped. His skull felt light, wreathed with algae. It took a moment for him to realize that his halo was gone. A line from Pushkin sprang to mind: *There is a memory of me, there is / In the world a heart in which I live.*

4

Celia del Pino

In which the lovers finally reunite as they once did . . . or do they?

Celia woke up the next morning in the immense hotel bed, nestled in Gustavo's arms. He was snoring operatically, his mouth open, a flourish of parsley on his teeth. Both of them were only partially clothed and the light filtering into their room was unforgiving. Celia took a quick inventory of her appearance. Her shoes were off, her blouse unbuttoned, her bra still fastened, though the straps had slipped off her shoulders. Her hair was in abject disarray.

Had something happened between them last night? Celia couldn't remember. Her head ached from an excess of wine and sherry and her belly was distended from the mountains of Andalusian food. There was a smoky, unidentifiable taste in her mouth. She vaguely recalled bingeing on oysters. The night had ended in the small hours, with Moorish meringues and a rousing rendition of "Granada" from the flamenco trio.

Celia disentangled herself from Gustavo and got a good look at him. His pants were off but his shirt was on and neatly buttoned. His striped boxer shorts and socks (held up by black garters) appeared undisturbed. He was collapsed onto his right side, one foot dangling off the bed, his bald head splotchy. His blue velvet slippers were on the floor, festooned with foppish ribbons. This wasn't how she'd imagined their first morning after. If, in fact, it was a morning after.

Coño, what a time for her memory to fail!

Celia fumbled over to the bathroom with its perplexing array of gadgets and caught a glimpse of herself in the mirror. Her eyes were smudged with mascara, her mouth greasily smeared with who knew what. Y, por dios, a thick hair was sprouting from the drooping mole on her jaw! She scrambled for her tweezers and plucked it out. One less embarrassing calamity. Celia pulled down her pantyhose—ripped from left hip to swollen knee—and lowered herself onto the toilet.

Afterward, curious about the bidet, she fiddled with its faucet handles and unleashed a jet of water that spectacularly hit the ceiling. ¡Carajo! She threw a few enormous towels on the mess, tiptoed to the balcony—so as not to wake Gustavo—and peeked through the curtains.

It was overcast and impossible to tell the time. The river below was muddy, sluggish. Did it flow into the Guadalquivir, of which García Lorca had so lovingly written? Along its banks were imposing willows and orange trees brimming with fruit. Footbridges crisscrossed the river from the Alhambra hillside to what looked like a warren of medieval alleyways. Was she imagining the Islamic call to prayer? Already, she'd spent a day and a night in Granada and had seen next to nothing.

A line from García Lorca came to mind: *mil violines caben en la palma de mi mano.* In 1930, Celia had heard the poet read in Havana at the Teatro Principal de la Comedia. Many in the audience recited his words along with him, which pleased the poet. But García Lorca soon grew serious, cautioning that fascist winds were blowing in Spain, and elsewhere. A free Cuba, he said, was more vital to the world than a rich Cuba—or even a safe one, if safety came at the cost of liberty. Celia joined the crowd in a standing ovation.

"Mi amor, ¿qué haces?" Gustavo asked, startling her. He was sleepy-eyed and propped up on one elbow. His head floated above the tide of disheveled sheets. "Ven aquí."

"I need a bath."

"It looks like you already had one."

"That damn bidet is lethal!"

"Shall we take a bath together, then?"

"No, we shall not," Celia said, and Gustavo laughed.

"How about a little breakfast, then?"

"I can't eat again for days."

"You're not one of those women who forswears food, are you? Who lives on air?"

"That's me. Living on air, living on dreams." Celia wanted to sound breezy but the words came out accusatorily. What was she doing here, anyway, so far from home? What had possessed her to open Gustavo's letter in the first place? Why had she allowed him to persuade her to undertake this pitiable journey? To steal what was left of her peace of mind?

Nostalgia was a vicious trap, she thought, its delusions an endless source of sorrow. Foolishness, pure foolishness, had brought her here! Hoy mismo she would pack up her red suitcase with its pathetic, hopeful contents and return home to her little brick-and-cement house by the sea, to her solitude and hard-won serenity.

"No te vayas, mi vida," Gustavo said, as if reading her mind. "Que te necesito." He kneeled before her with difficulty. The top of his skull was poignantly dappled with liver spots.

"Por favor, Gustavo." Celia held her breath to prevent the tears from falling. "I've said nothing of the sort."

"But I heard you nonetheless."

"Please get up. You're embarrassing me."

"That's all it takes?" Gustavo pushed himself back to standing with a groan. "Dance with me, corazón." He pressed his unshaven cheek to hers, humming and swaying to "Lágrimas Negras," their bolero son. His body felt light, barely there, as if his bones were made of aluminum.

"You're trembling," Celia whispered.

"It's my heart."

Celia laid her head on his chest. It was true. His heart was a tremolo of emotion.

"Aquí estamos, mi amor. For however long this moment lasts. When the world would have us preparing for death." Gustavo kissed Celia on the mouth. "Stay with me. I have another surprise for you."

"Your surprises will be the death of me!"

"Not this one, I promise." He trundled over to the armoire and extracted a musical instrument case, a tripod, and a collapsible stool. Gustavo set the case on the floor and snapped it open. There was a cello inside, burnished to gleaming.

"Have you hidden a musician in there, too?" Celia teased.

Gustavo smiled, tuned the strings with restrained fanfare, then picked up the bow. Celia sat on the edge of their bed, intrigued. When had he learned to play the cello?

"As you know, this was written for solo piano," he said. "But I had a composer friend adapt it for the cello."

With the opening notes, Celia recognized Debussy's "La Soirée dans Grenade." How could Gustavo have known what this music meant to her? How she'd played it incessantly in the early years of her marriage, when her health was delicate. How the doctors had warned her husband to keep her away from Debussy, fearing that the Frenchman's restless style might compel her to rashness. How Celia continued to play the piece when she was alone, daydreaming of meeting Gustavo on a moonlit riverbank, of making love under the watchful poplars of Granada, the air fragrant with jasmine and myrtle and citrus.

When Gustavo finished playing, she beckoned him to the bed. They sat and faced each other for a long moment. "Put your hands on me," Celia said. "It's time."

And so, very slowly, they began navigating their tangle of stiff limbs. The years, she realized, had mercifully erased most of the differences between them, smoothing their bodies to near-similarity. They caressed each other's aches and pains—his pulled calf muscle, the crick in her lower spine, his Achilles heel (brutally sliced in prison), her bursitic shoulder, the whitened scar where her breast used to be—gently coaxing long-hidden places to moistness.

Whenever one or the other apologized for clumsiness or inflexibility, insecurity or unsightliness ("Don't look there!"), they called out, "VANITAS VANITATUM!"—Gustavo started this game with much merriment—and retreated to the safety of eyes-closed bites and kisses.

Gradually, the memory of their younger bodies accommodated their older, more forgiving ones. They found accord in their flesh, in the frisson of unhurried gliding, surrendering to the exquisite, mutual ministrations of love.

As Celia felt herself releasing, she blindly reached between Gustavo's thighs but found it quiet there. Without embarrassment, he excused himself and re-emerged from the bathroom moments later, proudly ready.

When the lovers got stuck in an awkward position that required some maneuvering to undo, they renewed themselves with mineral water and tangerines. It was these tangerines that transported them to new heights of ecstasy. They sucked the segments from their lips, squirted juice down each other's throats, trailed bits of tangerines along their inner thighs. Neither wanted to stop, not knowing if this realm of flesh, this cosmos of pleasures, might ever, could ever, happen again.

And, defying time, they followed their bodies to rapture.

5

Ivanito Villaverde

Becoming La Lupe . . .

La Ivanita tasted the updated Cuban cocktail that the bartender brought her: aged rum, honey, bubbly water, fresh lime juice, and a dash of chili pepper. How it packed a blinding punch! The rum lubricated her strut across the dressing room on six-inch stilettos. Hip roll, hip roll, shimmy-shimmy, stop. The trick to performing La Lupe was timing her rare moments of stasis. If she managed to hit these just right, the show would catch fire.

Así, puro fuego.

La Ivanita stood before the gilded full-length mirror. A flawless diva looked back, stunning in a replica of the gold halter jumpsuit that had made Dick Cavett's jaw drop. She touched her image with reverence, then began clapping out the rhythm of la clave. La Lupe had grown up listening to its syncopations in every rumba, every conga, every son and guaracha—live, or recorded—in her hometown of Santiago de Cuba. In that city of carnivals, the drums were always beating.

The rain hadn't let up since noon, bejeweling the trees, flooding the streets. But her fans—many of them rival drag queens—weren't dissuaded. Opening night had sold out weeks ago, as had most of La Ivanita's month-long run at Chez Schatzi. Scalpers, she'd heard, were doing a brisk business with the line of hopefuls waiting to get inside. La Ivanita lit a votive candle, then sprinkled a few drops of her rum cocktail on the tiny santería altar. At its center was the photo of Mami on the beach, in a cowrie-shells frame.

The stage manager slid open the leather curtain and gave her a nod. It was time.

La Ivanita waited in the wings until the crowd was in a frenzy— shouting her name, stamping like a thousand La Lupes. Searchlights swiveled against the golden palettes of the club. As soon as she stepped onto the proscenium, a bouquet of long-stemmed white roses landed at her feet. Other bouquets came flying through the spotlight—gardenias, fire lilies, rainbow tulips trailing ribbons— scattering across the stage. *Ravish us, Queen! We love you! Bitte, don't be cruel, Gottin!*

The fans' impatience raced through her veins, but La Ivanita didn't move a muscle. She was at her most powerful in this pro-tracted moment before the first song. For a split second everything appeared minuscule, as if she were peering the wrong way through binoculars. Then select details in the audience grew sharp: the chalky pallor of an ex-lover lingering by the bar; a grinning Dag-mar, impeccably coiffed behind her cat-eye glasses; the artsy dykes in their signature monocles and bow ties—one with an Afghan hound—who never missed a show.

So many familiar faces under those Bauhaus chandeliers.

La Ivanita raised her arms to silence the fans. A hush descended. The waiters stopped circulating, the bartender froze. All eyes were on her—glittering, larger than life. Her family beamed at her from the third row: Pilar, Irina, Tereza, and darling Azul (the only child in the room) on the edge of his seat, his hair freshly combed.

Who knew what their bodies harbored of love, what each em-braced of life? Together they were discovering what was possible, the labyrinth of a common future. La Ivanita never expected this, and she was immeasurably grateful. Their love had begun with mutual recognitions that defied logic—rife with magic, anarchy, wonder, bitter clashes. Yet the cousins had seized the unexpected and become family.

Onstage, glamour and death remained synonymous. And there was only this instant that, like dying, lasted forever. Not even Mami could offer her that. La Ivanita waited for the diva's spirit to overtake her—legs, sex, heart, scorched throat. Only then did she open her mouth to sing, wild with joy.

Soy dueña del universo
Dueña del palmar y del mar
Dueña del sol, dueña del cantar . . .

PILAR'S
LAST PHOTO

Image #7: 1993

In the after-photograph, I've just given birth. Azul is in my arms, a blue knitted cap on his head. My face is puffy, my eyes bloodshot, my jaw sore from grinding down so hard. I'm euphoric, terrified, relieved, madly in love. A nurse snaps this picture at my request.

Fourteen hours earlier (no photo available), I swear my obstetrics team to a zero-epidurals policy. But as the contractions intensify—an uncharted cartography of pain—I break down and beg for drugs. Which, of course, they don't give me. When my contractions mysteriously cease, the doctor jump-starts more agony with intravenous Pitocin. It feels like depth charges in my womb. Is birth, I wonder, more painful than death?

I'm having a boy. His name is Azul after, well, every last shade of blue in Cuba. It's the only name I ever considered. His Japanese father is thousands of miles away in Yokohama—and promises to remain there. My mother offered to fly to L.A. for the birth but I said: *Over my dead body*. She retaliated by telling me (again) what a huge baby I was: *Over nine pounds, Pilar! ¡Un monstruo! You nearly broke me in two!*

I grit my teeth as riptides of pain sweep through me. I focus on banishing Mom from my consciousness, imagine her receding, growing smaller, insignificant, a vanishing blip. This puts me in synch with my savage contractions. I want to feel powerful, invincible, at the heart of the universe. But I feel none of these things.

In the final stretch, I bear down for all I'm worth and crack a back molar. A shimmering hummingbird hovers near my face. I wonder if it's Abuela Celia, waiting to get a glimpse of her first great-grandchild. It's probably the drugs, but who cares? It's the best hallucination ever. The hummingbird stays until the pain fades away and my son—Azul Puente-Tanaka—emerges into the light.

It's 5:17 a.m. And just like that, I'm a mother.

Acknowledgments

Infinite gratitude to Ellen Levine, who's championed my work from Day One. No one has supported me more. I'm *here* because you've always been *there*.

A huge thank-you to the magnificent Reagan Arthur, who helped make this book the very best it could be. And to the whole genius team at Knopf: Isabel Meyers, John Gall, Nicole Pedersen, Amy Edelman, Ellen Whitaker, and Gabrielle Brooks.

Special thanks to my dear stalwart readers—Alfredo Franco, Scott Brown, and Alexis Gargagliano—for their insights, suggestions, and encouragement.

Shout-out to my friends and fellow literary travelers: Chris Abani, Achy Obejas, Carolina De Robertis, Angie Cruz, Ana Menéndez, Bobby Antoni, Las Dos Brujas community, and many more.

Mil gracias to my daughter, Pilar, and to my husband, Gary, for an abundance of love and cheer along the way.

A Note About the Author

CRISTINA GARCÍA is the author of eight novels, including *Dreaming in Cuban, The Agüero Sisters, Monkey Hunting, A Handbook to Luck, The Lady Matador's Hotel, King of Cuba,* and *Here in Berlin.* She's also published several books for young readers, a collection of poetry, and two Latinx anthologies. García's work has been nominated for a National Book Award and translated into fifteen languages. She is a resident playwright at Central Works Theater in Berkeley, California, and has taught at universities nationwide.

cristinagarcianovelist.com

A Note on the Type

This book is set in the typeface Bertham Pro. Designed by American typographer Steve Matteson (b. 1965), Bertham Pro made its debut in 2009 and is a revival of Frederic W. Goudy's original version. Matteson produced this unique typeface and added bold, italic, and openface styles. Visually graceful, Bertham Pro is unmistakably American by design and reminiscent of the quality craftsmanship of the 1960s.

COMPOSED BY DIGITAL COMPOSITION,
BERRYVILLE, VIRGINIA

PRINTED AND BOUND BY BERRYVILLE GRAPHICS,
BERRYVILLE, VIRGINIA

DESIGNED BY BETTY LEW